Nailed Down

Nailed Down

CHELLE BLISS
EDEN BUTLER

Chapter One
Kane

"I am the storm."

The guy only blinked at me, a little boy staring at something he didn't seem able to place. "You're... Wait, what?"

It was a problem that reared its tiny head anytime the producers sent another intern to me. They tended to scare easy or, you know, not scare at all. Couldn't let that shit slide. This was especially the case with the ones who had a dad or granddaddy or, *Christ*, girlfriend's father who knew someone who knew someone in the damn business. Even if we were just a small DIY cable network show, we were still Hollywood-ish. That meant favors. That meant I got landed with punk interns who didn't know a wrench from a garden hoe.

"I asked what you do." The kid closed his mouth, eyebrows up, hidden behind those thick black frames he wore. I didn't need to look him over too closely. I'd figured out his type when he hurried onto the set and darted straight for me before I was able to get half a mug of coffee down my throat. He didn't need my attention, not this damn early. Not looking the way he did—stupid glasses he probably didn't need and a bowtie, a fucking green striped bowtie and suspenders, and it wasn't anywhere near Halloween, God help me.

Hipster bullshit. Hipster bullshit I didn't have time for.

"So, when you say you're the storm..."

Fingers tightening around my mug, I worked my jaw, ignoring the kid as Dale and Gin came onto the set, dropping an armful of cut 1x4s onto the wood subfloor. The sound moved around the wide-open cabin and echoing right against the framing and exposed windows.

"He's the storm," the kid told Dale, a pathetic, forced laugh flicking that waxed mustache of his against his bottom lip. "Can you believe that?"

Dale was Navy. Twelve years. I'd hired him four years back—he didn't have a daddy or buddy in the fancy producer's trailer. The guy was good and got the job because he knew his shit. We'd grabbed a few beers the night after his first day so he could ask questions. I gave all my crew that shot. One time, only one, to ask what they wanted about me. After that, curiosity was off the table.

Dale had gotten the measure of me after three pints of Guinness. But the hipster intern? Yeah. That wasn't going to happen.

"He is the fucking storm." Dale said that with a finality that made the intern frown. Had the kid staring between me, nursing my cooling dark roast, and Dale, glaring down at the kid, stare weaving over the damn bowtie, the thick, curled mustache before he flared his nostrils, disgusted.

"The storm, kid. That's Kane. He's a hurricane when we're on a deadline. He's a tsunami when we fuck up. And if you do that too much, he's a motherfucking typhoon. You either handle your shit or prepare for the storm."

Maybe it was Dale's voice—that "Don't. Just don't." vibe every SEAL threw off no matter how long they'd been out of the service, but that sage bullshit wisdom worked. The kid jumped up, hardly managed to bother with a nod at me before he followed after Dale, picking up his drill, tugging on a tool belt that dirtied his stupid hipster skinny jeans.

I downed the rest of my coffee, holding back a laugh when the kid threw a glance over at me then jerked his attention away as I pointed to myself, mouthed "the fucking storm," and shot him the bird.

Damn straight. New season, the whole of which we'd spend a few miles from the entrance to Mount Rainier National Park renovating a huge log cabin, and a brand-new intern to torture. Hell, it was stupid, but I didn't party like I used to. Had to find some kind of fun where I could.

I gave the kid a day, maybe two. Once he realized this gig wasn't grabbing coffee for the producers or standing in for the grips or camera people, once he realized there was a hell of a lot of work to do, then he'd get bored or scared and head out with his tail between his legs. Or suspenders. Or custom Converse.

Dale barked orders at the kid as Gin fought with Mario, the floor contractor. The general bustle of bullshit that came along with the setup the crew did for shooting got louder, the noise annoying, gearing up to piss me right off. And then, somewhere about an hour into our day, all that shit went quiet. It was a silence I was familiar with; had heard it years before when kids at school back in Seattle saw me for the first time after my old man took a dirt nap. Funny thing about death. People are sorry for you, but they feel compelled to ignore you. Someone you love dies, and the world acts like you were the one who bit it. They don't have a damn clue what to say. They only know they can't mention death or dying or how much it sucks. So, in general, you get the silent treatment because, bottom line, people are self-centered, graceless assholes. Anyway, that was the thought I had, the familiar silent sting I recognized when all the noise on the set went still.

It meant Kit was back.

The kid was the only one still yammering on. Hands around an extension cord, Hipster was boring

Gin stupid about some shit I didn't care enough to listen to. I only knew she was listening to him because she jabbed him in the rib as I walked through the set, bypassing gawking, awkward folk watching as Bill, our producer, spoke to Kit like she was a kid, not the talented badass host of our show. He was doing the bumbling, clueless shit. A glance around the set, the stares she got as she walked into the cabin, and I realized everyone did the same—stared and gaped and looked like assholes in the process.

She kept her dark gaze on the top of the cup of coffee she held, listening to Bill as he patted her shoulder, as he made pointless attempts to distract her from the suck she'd landed in.

"So, you...um...I..." Bill spoke in monosyllables, some freakish jackass language he clearly didn't have a handle on. "What I mean is..."

"Look," Kit said, waving off his muttering stupidity with a shake of her head. "I get that this is weird, and you don't know what to say, but I'm okay."

"You really don't have to be back yet, sweetheart." It was hard not to laugh at the glare on Kit's face. She thought Bill was some reject from the seventies no one had clued in to the notion that it was definitely not okay to pinch a woman's ass or call a professional "sugar" or "sweetheart." I mean, shit. He was from California. Not Georgia. There was zero excuse for the sweet talk.

"I'm fine," she mumbled, hid those two words behind a long drink from her Styrofoam cup, and kept her gaze downcast, stifling the glare I knew was there.

"Babe, I know it's been hard." Bill stood a little closer than I liked, and I thought about breaking it up, telling him to go fuck himself, but I knew Kit wouldn't appreciate the big brother shit. She wasn't a princess. She was a fucking general. She could cover her own ass.

"I know you and your cousin were close." Bill put that flabby arm around her, and Kit straightened her shoulders, taking a step to the right to slip out of his reach. "Losing someone you're close to, well, I can imagine."

"Can you?" She didn't wear a lick of makeup. The chicks in the back trailer with all the girl shit hadn't gotten to her yet, and still Kit looked like something out of a Zeffirelli film; young, vibrant, skin like silk, eyes large and dark. Her face was heart-shaped, cheekbones pronounced, russet-colored eyes round with large lids. I loved her big eyes, how dark they were, how she kept everything she thought right behind them, never letting anyone see what went on in her head. She was beautiful, shaped with tempting curves and an athletic build, but her legs were long, and her ass was plump and spectacular. She looked like she belonged on the side of a B-52 bomber, inspiring fighting men to keep at it, not on some small DIY program that only drunks coming in from partying and newborn parents saw at four a.m.

"If you need anything," Bill tried again, but Kit cut him off, directing a wide, toothy smile at him that held more cyanide than sweetness behind it.

"Thank you, Bill. Really. And thank you for the flowers. They were nice." Then Kit grabbed his hand, dropping it from her shoulder. "But the only thing I want to do is get to work."

The quiet kept on, with the crew puttering with busywork shit that didn't need handling, all in weak attempts to watch Kit and Bill. It pissed me off, especially when those nosy assholes kept at their staring even when I stepped into the center of the room.

To my left, Kit was squaring off at Bill, challenging him with a glare to get any closer to her. She might not need me to do the big brother bullshit, but the crew did need reminding there was work to be done.

"Enough of this!" I shouted, not bothering to keep the bite out of my tone. "Get back to work." That staring moved from Kit and lingered on me, but only until I moved up an eyebrow and shouted, "Now!"

They scattered like a bunch of ants whose hill had been kicked by a mean fourth grader, but at least they got moving. Kit came at me a half a second later, standing at my side while she looked over the cabin. Two slow sips from her cup and one swipe of her gaze up to the roof and she finally spoke.

"You get the new header?"

I watched right along with her, pushing back the slow whiff of something sweet I caught coming from her hair. "Be here on Thursday. First thing in the morning." We stood there for several long seconds just watching the room, taking in the exposed beams and the looping wire curling through the walls. I could almost hear the gears in her head shifting, like she had something to say but didn't need me to fish it out of her.

When she went on drinking her coffee, I answered the questions she didn't voice but knew she had. "That shop in Shelton had your stove." She looked up at me then, and I thought I could make out a slow-working grin moving the side of her mouth. The woman liked her appliances. The older, the better. "It's a 1930 Aga. Black with copper fixtures. Fully restored."

Kit turned then, full smile now, and I shifted a glance down at her, head shaking at the flash of something ridiculous and fucking sweet in her eyes. "Stupid expensive?"

"Obscene."

That smile was lethal now, and if she'd been a less classy chick, I'd have sworn she was about to shimmy. Can't say I'd hate seeing that. "And Bill knows how much it was and still let you buy it?"

I shrugged, then nodded a thanks when Gin paused near us, close enough to hand over a refill on my coffee. She turned to Dale, offering him the same, and I cocked an eyebrow at the look he gave her. "I was convincing."

"Ha. You were intimidating," Kit said, nudging me with an elbow. "Thanks. That makes me happy."

"It's why I'm here." I hid the smug grin I wore behind my coffee, telling myself it wasn't stupid to feel like a chump for making the woman happy. I liked when she was happy. Mainly I liked being the man to do the job, but that shit came from somewhere I didn't bother thinking about. No need to imagine things when I knew the truth: Kit Carlyle was my friend, but fuck, did I want to be a helluva lot more than that.

"I don't know what I'd do without you," she admitted, and some stupid, ridiculous thing in my gut went all wobbly. But if Kit noticed the break in my composure—and the quick blink of my eyes and a long, slow sip from my mug to keep me from saying something stupid—she didn't mention it. Instead, she looked around the cabin, nodding a greeting to Gin when she smiled as she moved past us before I felt another nudge on my arm. "I need to run something by you."

"Such as?" But she went all quiet again, out of character when Kit wanted something, enough that I turned to watch her, eyebrows shooting up when she cast a look all around, looking damn guilty or stupid nervous. I couldn't tell which. "Something up?"

"Well, it's just that I need..."

"Hey, *Mr. Storm*..." The intern started laughing at himself before Kit stepped back, clearing her throat as though she didn't want this little punk to know she was about to say something only for my ears. That just pissed me off.

"You see me standing here speaking to someone?" I asked the kid, tilting my head to glare at him. He nodded, then looked to Kit as though she might tell him it was okay to interrupt us. But the woman's attention was on her phone when she took it out as a distraction. I snapped my fingers, bringing the kid's attention back to me. "Go. Away."

"Look, Kane..." But Hipster didn't get a chance to bug me any further. Dale approached, taking the kid's shoulder to turn him, then gave the boy a gentle shove to lead him back toward a stack of 1x4s. The saws started up after that, and I nodded toward the door, getting Kit to follow me out of the cabin and down the driveway until we were at my silver F-150. She hopped right in when I opened the door for her, curling her arms over her chest as though she were frozen solid. The woman was always cold, no matter the temperature, and always bitched that I never ran the heat in my truck.

"All right," I said, my head shaking at how she blew on her fingers like we were in the Arctic and not in a small wooded area intersected by Copper Creek. "Jesus." Then I flipped on the heater and moved the vents toward her. "Now. Whatcha got?"

"Oh." Kit went a little shy on me, way out of character, and I forgot about everything else but the small slip of fear that started crowding my head. This woman never shied away from telling me what to do or what she needed and the fact she wouldn't look at me put me on edge.

"Hey," I said, leaning over my steering wheel and moving my head toward her, trying to catch her attention. "What's wrong?"

"Nothing... It's just..." She exhaled and rubbed her eyes. I could make out the frown behind her hands when she scrubbed her face, and for some reason, that bullshit worry grew more intense. Finally, through a long breath, Kit looked at me straight on, licking her lips like I'd seen her do a thousand times. That shit meant trouble. I'd seen it firsthand. That slow, preparing for battle lip lick meant shit was about to get twisted. "Kane," she said, squaring her shoulders, "I need you. I need only you."

Fuck me, I was in trouble.

Chapter Two

Kit

"**M**s. Carlyle."

Sunshine splintered off the top of the black lacquer box, scattering in different directions, and I winced against the glare. Everything around me, including the man at my side, sounded dull and distant. I felt trapped in this endless tunnel, surrounded by people I didn't know on a day I'd prayed would never come.

The crowd was thinning, most of the other mourners already driving away without so much as a backward glance, heading to a party Jess had planned in the event, obnoxious as it sounded, of her untimely death. That bitch planned everything in detail, even what happened the day of her funeral. I wasn't following the rules, no matter how much I loved my cousin. I just couldn't find the strength to walk away.

"I was good friends with your cousin, ma'am."

I nodded but couldn't bring myself to look at him or reply.

A fresh wave of tears burned my eyes as I watched that black casket. Inside was my cousin, my best friend, and my mind could not organize thoughts and meaning with reality. She just couldn't be gone.

The man hovered, rearranging his feet, but otherwise, didn't bother me. He seemed to know I needed a second to myself.

Jess was the type of person people flocked to with her intoxicating laugh and charming smile. She never said a bad word about anyone and went out of her way to make those around her happy. The number of people who stood around her casket today was a testament to her character and infectious nature. Hell, even as a kid I was drawn to her.

The wind kicked up, blowing my hair into my face, and I rubbed my eyes, irritated that I couldn't keep from crying. But then, who could after their best friend died?

Growing up, I followed Jess around like a lost puppy dog. She never once shooed me away or treated me like her little cousin, never once told me I was a nuisance for following behind her and emulating her every move. We grew older, and the age gap seemed to fade, and then we became closer than sisters.

We were both alone and only had each other to lean on. Her parents passed in a tragic plane crash when she was in college, and my mother died a few years back from a sudden heart attack due to an undiscovered heart condition. We had no other family anymore except each other.

The man at my side cleared his throat, probably tired of my quiet sniffling, and the noise brought my attention back to him. He had long, straight fingers with trimmed nails that I noticed when he offered me a plain white envelope. "She wanted me to give this to you."

The envelope had Jess's neat, looping scribble on the front, but I couldn't see any more than that in my peripheral vision, and I was still too numb to move much more than my eyes. I was struck dumb, zoning out on anything but the twist of the flower stem between my fingertips, even as it started to bruise from the movement. I couldn't bring myself to let the calla lily go and place it on her casket with the others. The act was too final, too absolute. Letting it go meant she was gone, and reconciling that with reality just wasn't happening yet.

"I promised her I would make sure you received this."

Slowly, I dragged my gaze to his hand, spotting the crisp envelope he held between his fingertips. That scroll was clearer now, with "Kit Kat" across the front. She'd even written the little heart over the "I" like she always did.

He pushed the envelope closer, slipping it between my fingertips. "I'm sorry for your loss," he said as my gaze swept to meet his. His eyes were red and puffy, similar to my own, I'd guess. That happened when you'd been crying nonstop for a solid week.

"Sorry for your loss" was a weird expression I never understood. We lost things like purses, phones, and keys, but a person was never really lost. Jess was in that polished black casket covered in white calla lilies a foot from me. She wasn't lost. Losing a person wasn't the right term. It seemed so vague, so empty.

The envelope crinkled as I gripped the pristine paper in my palm. "Who are you?"

The man's gaze dropped to the ground as his Adam's apple bobbed, hiding beneath the collar of his dress shirt. "I'm Luke. Jess and I were..." He let the explanation die, shutting his eyes, and his features transformed, as though the thought of what they'd been was just too painful to explain at the moment. Finally, he exhaled, his expression relaxing before he said, "We were lovers."

It hit me then, looking at that handsome face. Despite the sadness of the day, the left side of my mouth twitched, recalling the things Jess mentioned about this man. She'd told me more than should have been allowed via text or email. Jess met Luke at a bar one night after work over six months ago, and their relationship moved fast, oftentimes too quick for Jess.

"Jess spoke highly of you." My voice didn't sound like my own. The flat, lifelessness monotone words slipped from my tongue as if there were someone else speaking through me.

Luke wiped the tears from his cheek, the back of his hand damp, and his cuff darkened with the motion. "I loved her, you know."

"I know." I knew more than I ever wanted to know about Luke. My cousin had made sure of that. Jess didn't keep a single fact from me, including the precise curve and girth of his penis, down to his favorite position during sex. She overshared, but I never stopped her. My insanely busy work schedule kept me off the market, and I was left letting my fantasies come alive vicariously through Jess's filthy, filthy sexual encounters with Luke.

"I thought we'd get married." That seemed to pain him more than admitting he loved her, and I brushed his arm, squeezing it once.

Her free, never-settle spirit and the burden of young loss would have likely hurt Luke, considering she might have turned him down. But then, Jess confessed that Luke was the first man who had her questioning her choice never to get attached. I understood her logic, knew it far too well. But with that loner decision came the loneliness. There was only so much work you could do to fill up your day.

Luke cleared his throat again, reminding me he was still there, and I glanced at him, forcing a weak smile as I looked back down at the casket. "I think you were the one person who could've made Jess change her mind."

"I had a ring and was going to propose on her birthday."

I jerked my head up fully, and something quickened in my chest. The stabbing pain that had replaced my heart intensified. "I'm sorry." I swallowed hard as the tears I'd thought had dried up blurred my vision.

"She has it now," he whispered, shaking his head as he inhaled. "I have to go. I can't stand here anymore. It hurts too much." He stepped back, his face contorted into something that made him look equal parts devastated and furious, and then Luke walked away.

But I stayed where I stood, my feet rooted next to Jess. Despite the reason for being here, I didn't want to leave and couldn't make myself go. The thought of leaving her, of walking away, was far sadder than staying here with her.

A worker moved in my direction wearing chunky work boots covered in mud and his hands tucked into his pockets, trying not to stare. "Ma'am, we were just about to close her up."

"Can I have ten more minutes, please?" I begged.

"Sure," he said as his gaze lingered a little too long. Maybe he knew my face but couldn't place how he knew me, which was often the case with my being on late-night television.

Kneeling on the ground, I clutched the envelope and flower in my hands, my attention on the casket. "Jess," I whispered. "I don't know how to do life without you." Tears slid down my cheeks, dropping to the bottom of my black dress. "You can't leave me like this."

The sadness morphed then, became something overwhelming, something that felt like a weight heavy on my chest. She was gone. With the snap of my finger, the blink of my eye, my best friend, my only family was gone. That sadness changed my cry; it grew, mingled into a guttural sob, and I became breathless, the grief hitting me in waves, growing with each second.

"Why?" I asked the sky above me, feeling helpless, faithless, wondering if whatever higher power that was up there could hear me. If it cared at all that my heart was breaking. "Fucking why?"

The flower broke in two as I doubled over, hands on my face. The stem bent in my palm, brittle now as the delicate white top tumbled to the grass. The envelope bit into my flesh, reminding me I still had one final piece of Jess left.

The heavy scent of her perfume caught on the breeze when I tore into the envelope and pulled out the soft pink pages. There was a crinkle in the center, but I'd managed not to damage the letter too badly. I was hungry for her words, desperate for this last connection to Jess. I scanned the black ink, flipping

*through the pages, wishing there were more. I took
a deep breath and blinked a few times and read the
first line.*

My Kit Kat,

If you're reading this, that means I've kicked it.
God, that must suck. Hopefully, I went out naked,
orgasming so hard my brain melted. Possibly with a
bottle of Jack in one hand and my fingers nestled in
Luke's deliciously wavy hair as he kneeled in front
of me and... Well. I'll try to retain some semblance
of dignity seeing as how these are probably my last
words.

"Here lies Jessica. She died with a stupid grin on
her face."

Sorry, couldn't resist.

If I have indeed bitten it, there are things I want to
say to you. I won't go on and on and write a monologue
that is profound and tear-jerking because that's not
who we are, is it? We live to laugh and laugh to live.
It's how we've survived. But I will tell you the single
most important thing I can...the thing I've wanted to
tell you for a long damn time. The thing I worried you
would never figure out on your own. So, here goes:

Kathryn Carlyle, life isn't a dress rehearsal, and
you're stuck backstage.

I say this with love. I say it because I've watched
you spend the past five years of your life working and
plotting and generally making everyone else's life

beautiful. Meanwhile, you stay in that tiny rental, miles from the most beautiful mountain in the world, nursing a pint of Ben & Jerry's (Don't deny it. I'm the one who turned you on to Half Baked) petting your Himalayan tom who is so fucking Gandalf-old he doesn't meow, he grumbles, and not once have you done anything remotely exciting with your life. Seriously, you are the only human person alive who can land a cable show and never show up to any of the fancy Hollywood bigwig, kiss your ass, oh aren't you fabulous, shindigs they always invite you to. Is that little cabin really that appealing?

You start project after project with the best of intentions and never finish them. I dare you to peek into your craft/storage/work-out room without having even the smallest amount of guilt.

I won't even discuss the below-average sex you've had and how long it's been since even those pathetic activities have happened.

You are dynamic and beautiful and funny and brilliant and so criminally talented, and the sad thing is you don't know it. Not really. You can make a shack look like Shangri-la, but you live in so much fear that you have no idea how old you're becoming and how quickly that's happening.

Kit Kat, it's time to live.

I love you, and because I do, I'm giving you a gift. It was something I gave to myself ten years ago when I wasn't all that dissimilar from you. When I was so scared of everything out there in life that I wasn't really living at all.

This is your bucket list. If you love me, ever really loved me, then you will complete everything on this list. It's my last wish. My final say-so. The last bossy thing I'll ever say to you, but it's the most important.

Life is a journey, and you haven't even gotten out of bed.

Time to pack your bags and get started.

Don't be sad that I'm gone, Kit Kat. Be happy I lived and loved while I was here.

I'll be watching.

Jess

"Shit," I said, trying not to laugh at my cousin as I kneeled next to her casket, her list of demands between my fingers. Wondering how in the hell I could pull this off. "Double shit."

The ever-present crease between Kane's eyebrows deepened as he stared at me, blinking slowly like I hadn't just word-vomited a shitload of information his way. "Say that again."

This time, when I explained the letter, I talked slowly, hoping he caught on to the detail I gave. Wasn't like it was difficult, but I wasn't about to comment on that. Not to him. Not when he looked like I had spiders crawling out of my eyes.

My dilemma explained, I smiled, hoping the big guy would think I was moderately cute, maybe feel bad for me because, clearly, I was still consumed by grief and not thinking rationally. "So, I need your help," I told him as I rubbed my hands together as close to the vent as I could get. "You game?"

Kane tightened his grip on the steering wheel, blinking like he still didn't quite get what favor I'd asked as he stared at me. "I don't know how I can help."

Leaning forward, I reached into my back pocket and fished out the letter before pushing it toward his face. "Read it. I can't do all this stuff by myself. I need a wingman."

He stared at the paper like it was going to jump up and bite him. "So, you want me to be your wingman."

Seriously, it wasn't difficult, but I pushed a smile onto my face, this one wider, and nodded toward the letter in his big hands. Kane was fearless; he never quit a job once he started it. I needed him to help me when I chickened out on completing Jess's list. And I knew I would. She wasn't wrong. I'd start but rarely end things I wanted for myself.

Kane squinted, and the same, "What shit does she want me to do?" look crossed his face before I cocked an eyebrow. With a little prodding, I'd get him to agree. I always could.

"Read it. Stop being a punk."

He snatched the paper from my fingers, black eyes on me as he unfolded the sheets. "You sure you want me to read this?"

"Yes." I sighed and rolled my eyes, pushing the paper closer to him.

He leaned against the window, facing me as his eyes moved across the page. "I don't know about this," he said, glancing over the paper at me with uneasiness.

"Did you read it all?"

"Not yet."

"Keep going."

His profile was striking. Kane had always had the face of someone fierce. All those hard edges, all the strict discipline he used in his life—managing the crew and construction on set or handling his brother, all the work he did in the gym or on the track—showed on his angular face. His lips were large, wide, and he had a deep crease in his cupid's bow. But his eyebrows were on the heavy side, making him seem dangerous, and there was always a smattering of stubble, all jet black, on his chin. Kane had wide shoulders, big hands, and thick thighs and not an ounce of fat on him. He reminded me of someone ancient, old features you'd see in black-and-white pictures in history books. His skin was dark and smooth, probably both from the amount of time he spent in the sun and the rich heritage given to him by his Samoan family. He was proud of who he was and where he came from, something I'd always admired about him.

I had a pulse. I was a woman. No way anyone could look at Kane and not see how rugged, how beautiful he was. Even me, his platonic friend.

He went still, quiet, his eyes rounding, narrowing, then growing huge again as he read, and I knew why. There was shit on that list Kane would flat out refuse to help me with because, well, that was Kane. That list scared me too. Kane took a breath, released it, then flipped the first sheet over and continued reading Jess's last words that were only meant for me.

Jess's Final Say-So:
Ten Things Kit Must Do Without Question:
1. *Go zip-lining - conquer your fear of heights, you little chicken.*
2. *Buy something frivolous, and I don't mean ice cream - See my stash in the closet safe. You know the combination. $1500 minimum.*
3. *Go Whale Watching - Because I know you're stupid for them.*
4. *Find someone to give you a mind-numbing, toe-curling, can't breathe, moan-worthy kiss that ruins you for all other men.*
5. *Run the half marathon you keep saying you want to train for.*
6. *Shake hands with the president.*
7. *Camp out in the mountains - no RVs or campers allowed.*

8. *Sing in front of a crowd of more than twenty people.*
9. *Have sex with someone other than yourself.*
10. *Fall in love.*

One wide eye shot at me, and Kane folded the letter in half, shoving it back at me like he couldn't get it out of his hands fast enough. "Sorry, Kit. Can't help you."

"What?"

"I just can't." He was out of his truck, door shutting closed before I could stop him. I grabbed his keys, trailing behind him as he stomped back toward the cabin.

He wore a worn, brown Carhartt jacket that was thick and scratchy, and I managed to grab the point of his elbow, pulling him back before he made it too far from the truck. "What exactly do you mean, you can't?"

I'd never heard Kane say those words. Even the most impossible designs, the most elaborate architectural elements he'd take on, never batting an eye even if he'd never attempted it before. "Can't" wasn't in the man's vocabulary. But there it was, flying right past his full lips all rude and obnoxious.

"The answer's no, Kit." He stalked across the yard, gaze on the cabin as I shook his keys at him, trying to get him to stop.

"Kane!" I yelled, stunned and a little pissed off.

He raised his hand high in the air but kept marching toward the cabin. "Nope. Can't do it."

"What the fuck?"

With my hands at my sides, I strode across the yard, making my way to the cabin in half the steps I normally took just to keep up with him, and nearly crashed through the closed door.

Kane had already forgotten me and my request, had busied himself by torturing the new intern with the dumb suspenders, bellowing orders and demands in a tone that told me Kane was lashing out, avoiding even looking in my direction.

It took a few minutes of deep breathing and waving my assistants off as they fluttered around me to get my irritation under wraps. I still couldn't keep the small curl from my mouth as I gave them one-word answers. Kane went back to work, hazarding small glances my way, but he wouldn't look directly at me.

"Sweetheart, you okay?" Bill asked, interrupting the perfectly good glare I was giving Kane as I debated walking right up to him and demanding he explain this foreign "can't" word of his. Bill gave me the creeps, was a little too touchy-feely for my taste, and I stepped back, diverting the brush of his hand on my shoulder as he smiled at me. That look was condescending, a little pitying, and it pissed me off. "You look frazzled."

"I need to talk to Kane."

"You don't need Kane. Let *me* help," Bill said, his voice gentle, utterly annoying as he managed to rest his hand on my shoulder. "I'm a good listener."

Kane shot another glance at me, this one landing as he spotted Bill, looking at him, then me. Kane hated Bill more than saying "can't." They were oil and water but somehow coexisted for the sake of the show. It was no surprise when Kane pushed the folder in his hand to Gin and stepped toward us

"Maybe you can help," I said loud enough that I knew Kane would overhear.

I repressed a shudder when Bill moved his hand from my shoulder to my neck and started to knead my muscles. "I'm your man, babe."

Every time he called me "babe," "sweetheart," or some other demeaning nickname, I had to restrain myself from kicking him in the balls. He was only palatable in small doses because Kane was always there to make sure Bill kept his ass in line.

I peeked over his shoulder, and like clockwork, Kane's steps got quicker, his features sterner, his fists clenched tightly at his sides.

"Well…" I started to say, stalling because I wanted to wait to see if Kane would take my bait.

Kane loomed over Bill, standing at his back with his arms crossed. "It's fine," he said, voice low, dangerous, and I had to push back the small thrill that shot through my stomach at the sound. "You're not needed, Bill."

Bait taken. Mission accomplished.

Chapter Three

Kane

Kit made a damn list. On top of the one left to her by her dead cousin. A list of the list *and* a fucking schedule. I was tempted to crumple "my copy" between my fingers as I glanced down at it.

"This will keep us on schedule. Every weekend that we don't film. Without fail until the list is done. Agreed?"

I'd half expected her to spit in her hand before she offered it to me for a shake. But Kit was funny, not goofy, and though the list was damn redundant, it somehow made her feel better. I had gotten a little freaked when I read that stupid list. Especially when it came to the kiss and the sex part. I couldn't get my head wrapped around the last item.

Fall in love.

Fuck me.

The low grunt I made must have alerted the waitress, and the tiny redhead turned toward me, a ready grin waiting as she pushed a hip against her tray.

"You want another one, gorgeous?" She took my nod, offering a wink that made her heavily wrinkled eyelid twitch, and then sashayed away. Crystal. Good lady. The sort of woman who had spent a lifetime slinging beer in the shiftiest looking water holes imaginable. But this place, Lucky's, had been my home away from home since we got stuck in Ashford for this project. The town was nice enough, but small. Nothing like the life I led in Tacoma or even Seattle, where I grew up. But Lucky's had a good staff, and the lights were low. Worked wonders when you wanted to keep a low profile.

"Why are you sulking?"

Home away from home, but not away from my brother.

"Don't start," I told him, pushing his chair back when he hovered too long. Crystal set a Guinness in front of me, then squinted at my brother. The asshole smiled, standing too close to the old lady, but she didn't back down.

"I guess you want that domestic shit? Bud or Miller?"

"I'm a Blue Moon man, actually." Kiel laughed at the waitress when she clicked her tongue at him, disgusted, walking behind her a half a step as she headed toward the bar. "Crystal, run away with me. I'll treat you so good." He thought a lot of himself, hitting on anything that wiggled just right. But Crystal wasn't buying it. She shot Kiel the finger, calling him something not many would have the stones to as she disappeared toward the cooler.

"Leave the old woman alone and sit." He caught the chair when I pushed it again with my foot, but he sat down, still laughing to himself. "Why are you here?" He never left Seattle if he could help it, and Ashford wasn't exactly some hopping bedlam for pretty boys like Kiel.

"What?" my brother said, faking a concerned frown. That asshole wasn't concerned about anything but landing a story that would put his byline front and center of the *Seattle Times*. Still don't know how the hell he'd managed to land that gig. "I can't check in on my big brother?"

"Not unless you want something."

He waved me off. "On my way to Portland for a story. Thought I'd check up on you."

When Crystal appeared again, not bothering to give more than an eye roll to Kiel as she slid the Blue Moon in front of him, I kicked his leg, knowing he was about to fuck with the old lady again.

She was halfway to the bar before my brother ignored my warning glare and called over his shoulder, "Where's my orange slice?"

Crystal didn't miss a beat, yelling back, "Up your ass, bitch," before she tended to the group of dockworkers who'd entered.

"I don't get why she doesn't like me," he said, grumbling a little while he downed his punk beer. "I'm way manlier than you are and not nearly as mean."

"Whatever you gotta tell yourself."

He watched me closely, leaning over the table as he scratched a line with his thumb into the label. I knew I should have expected the question before it came, but it still took me by surprise that my brother could do the job he did and still have no clue how to read me.

"Dude, you look like shit." He moved back against the table, pulling on his beer. "You still moping about Kit being gone?" Kiel shifted in his chair, eyebrows shooting up when I ignored him. "She's still out?"

"She's back," I said, my gaze shifting around the bar to the dockworkers hassling Crystal for taking too long with their order. My attention was on alert, sharp as the biggest of the workers yelled something rude at Crystal because his beer wasn't cold enough. "Got back today."

Kiel followed my stare, swinging his legs around as though he was ready to pounce if those assholes got to be more than the old waitress could handle, but my kid brother was clueless.

"Easy," I told him, shaking my head. "She can handle that shit."

And before the words had left my mouth completely, Crystal had an empty bottle in her hand, raising it overhead when the dockworker grabbed her arm. He had enough time for a cool, vicious curl to move her top lip before she knocked the jackass across the face.

"Out!" she called, clearing the bar top as the guy's friends helped him to his feet. "Right now, assholes, and don't come back!" Crystal was little, but loud and scary as hell. I was a big dude, but I still knew better than to mess with her.

"Told you," I said, giving the old waitress a nod of approval as she glanced in our direction.

Kiel went white, and when the old lady stared at him, my brother turned around, suddenly interested in his Blue Moon.

"So," he tried, "you look like shit because..."

I knew I couldn't divert him for long, but I didn't want to cry into my beer, blabbering to my kid brother about Kit and the shit she wanted from me. I kept what I thought locked down tight. Kiel was slick, always had some woman on the side because he was a good-looking dude and he could talk a preacher into a porno subscription. But he was nothing like me. We looked alike, had the same wide frame, the same high cheekbones and mouths that stretched across our faces, even the same thick, unruly hair, though Kiel knew how to work his. I just kept mine short. But Kiel was smooth, gave a shit about what he wore, what label was on his clothes, when I was good with Levis and flannels. But how we lived, what we cared about, or what mattered to us? Nah, that's where we differed.

"She's got a bucket list she wants help with," I finally told him, ignoring the slow grin that moved across his mouth.

"And what's on this list?"

I waved him off, sighing hard when that grin turned into something ridiculous that made him look like the fucking Joker. "Shit she wants to do." Kiel went on smiling, that expression fracturing only a little as he shifted his weight against his elbows. He'd do that shit forever—watch, waiting for me to fess up. The jackass had the patience of a priest, and when he went on gawking, expecting, I decided to give up a little of what was bothering me. Shoulders lowering, I downed the last of my Guinness and pushed the glass aside. "Fine. On that list is shit that could make things...complicated."

"Ah," he said, crossing his arms as he watched me. "Like sex things." I grunted but didn't confirm a thing. "And no matter how many times you hand me that bullshit about not wanting anything with her, I'm not blind. You get that look anytime she's around."

"What look?" The guy was off his meds or something. Like I said, I kept everything locked down, even how I looked at her.

"Dude, give me a break." Kiel shook his head, pulling a mint from the roll in his pocket. He'd stopped smoking five years back but still needed the mints to do something with his hands. "Kit comes around, and that grumpy-ass frown on your face vanishes. You look at her like you're lost in the desert and she's just the right amount of wet that will quench your thirst."

Another grunt, but this time, I shot a glare at my brother for mentioning shit that shouldn't be in his mouth. He shrugged when I flipped him off, but he didn't give me hell about Kit.

"So you wanna help her out, but you think things will get...iffy?"

My brother had a way with words, no shit there. But I still didn't want him knowing what was in my head. I damn well didn't want anyone to know. "Something like that," I finally admitted, figuring he'd badger me until I gave up even the smallest detail.

Kiel nodded, moving his lips together like he needed to smear the words around before he set them loose. Then, he snapped his fingers, like he'd just come up with some grand idea that was the greatest shit any bastard ever thought up. "Distract her."

"And how should I go about that shit?"

"There aren't any rules about what gets done first, are there?"

Kit hadn't mentioned it, though if I knew her, and God help me I did, she'd be a stickler for staying in order. "No, but she'll probably..."

Kiel waved his hand, shutting me up. "You can distract anyone, man. You're a bully when you want to be, when it's something you want. And if I'm hearing you right, what you want is to keep what you're thinking about her out of the equation."

"Fuck you, I'm not a bully." It was insulting for him to say shit that wasn't true. But then Kiel leaned back, stretching his long legs out in front of him as he shook his head, and a quick flash of stupid shit I'd done as a kid came back to me. "Locking you in the girls' bathroom freshman year taught you a lesson."

"I got suspended."

"Yep, but did you ever try sneaking peeks at the girls' shower after that?" He didn't respond, and I took that as denial. "Thought so, asshole. Shit I did was to keep you in line."

"Never mind that," Kiel said, avoiding Crystal as she walked around the tables, cleaning up the mess left over from the afternoon crowd. "Distract her. It'll buy you some time until you figure out what you wanna do."

"Nothing to do," I told him, moving my hand to the exit to signal Crystal to close out my tab. "What kind of bullshit friend won't help out when she's just lost her best friend in the world?"

"The kind that doesn't want her to know he's gone all stupid for her."

I stuffed my card into my wallet when Crystal laid the bill on the table and scribbled my name and a hefty tip on the bill. "Not stupid," I told Kiel, ignoring his low laugh. "Just...a little dumb." That was the word that best described how Kit made me feel. Dumb. Awkward, a little helpless, and I hated feeling that shit. As my brother nodded at Crystal, this time neglecting to make a smartass comment or flirt with her, I followed him to the door, waving at the old waitress with my head full of stuff that might work as a distraction. I only hoped Kit would be down for avoiding shit I just wasn't ready to deal with.

Chapter Four

Kane

"Nope. Nope... Changed my mind."

I had a feeling Kit would chicken out. She did that a lot. The woman was full of great intentions but not much on the follow-through. I knew her limits. I knew when to push and when to back away. You couldn't be friends with someone, work with them as closely as we had for the past five years, and not know how to read them or figure out when their limits were met.

Her running away from the suspension bridge, that stupid hard hat and the goggles on top of it jostling as she walked back toward the gate, told me Kit's limit wasn't quite in the rearview, but it was inching closer.

"Hang on a second, you crazy woman." Three long strides and I caught up to her, touching her arm to get her to stop. Her eyes were wide, a little frantic, and for a second I wondered if she'd bother to blink before the tears started to form. "You told me this was okay, remember? You told me you wanted to get this one over with."

There was a small crowd and a few stragglers who must have recognized us. But the thing about Ashford was that even local celebrities, for the most part, got left alone. One, maybe two double takes, then Kit and I were on our own, secluded a bit by a large Douglas fir tree with browning leaves and heavy limbs. Overhead, though, there were high-pitched screams releasing, muffling, and turning into shit that sounded like something from a horror flick as the zip-liners took off from the deck at the top of the suspension bridge and shot away going at least thirty-five miles per hour.

Kit took her wide, scared gaze from my face, finally blinking, lashes moving like a hummingbird's wings as one particularly loud zip-liner screamed at the top of her lungs, "Holy shit, someone stop!"

"Oh, hell no!" Kit yelled, stepping back and away from me as she kept her gaze on the screaming woman overhead. "Fuck that!"

"Calm down," I told her, blocking her when she tried hightailing it away from the bridge. "Would you listen for a second?" She skirted around me, like a damn ball player readying a lay-up, but I kept up with her, managing to spread my arms to keep her from hitting the narrow trail that led to the parking lot. "Shit, woman, you're acting ridiculous."

"Move, Kane. I changed my mind. I can't do this. It's..." She threw another glance up toward the zip line, then took to shaking her head, repeating "Nope, nope, no" under her breath. "No way. I just... I can't..."

"Stop right there," I told her, not moving. I made my features tighten, shot her the frown I knew she hated. That disappointed tension on my face usually showed up when the PAs or interns got on my nerves or when Bill wanted the impossible and my crew couldn't deliver. Kit had always mentioned how that expression made me look vicious and mean. I didn't want her to see it, but I'd made her a promise. We shook on it, and I kept my word when I gave it. "You wanted my help. You wanted me to push you, remember?"

She swallowed, and the smallest line moved between her eyebrows, like she was only just remembering the deal we'd made. "But, Kane..."

"Your cousin knew you could do it, Kit. She wanted you to." I stepped closer, not liking the shake in her fingers or how every time a loud shriek sounded overhead, Kit scrunched up her face, wincing like the sound hurt her. "It was her last wish, right?"

The blink was slow, and when she moved her lids up, I caught the gold flecks that glinted against the sunlight in her big eyes. "Low blow, Kane."

I shrugged, not remotely sorry for playing the dead cousin card. "Come on." I turned her around, resting a hand against the small of her back in case she thought of taking off again. "I promise, I won't let anything happen to you."

The nerves must have kept her silent, because Kit didn't speak as we navigated the hike toward the bridge, then the thin, swinging rope itself. She made white-knuckle grips against the twisted railing, footsteps heavy and sure as she walked in front of me.

"Few more feet," I told her, holding back a laugh when she nodded her head, a quick affirmative motion that made her long hair slap against her face. "You're okay."

Around us, the tall trees seemed to stretch on forever. There were huge clusters of limbs and branches that reminded me of the tree house Kiel and I built when we were fifteen so our little cousin Shawna could have camp-out sleepovers with the other eight-year-olds in the neighborhood. It had taken us a solid month to finish it, and I did most of the work myself, but when it was done, Shawna spent every night that summer sleeping under the stars. Her smile alone was worth the work we put into it.

Kit, though, was making me doubt the wisdom of agreeing to the bargain. She really was a chickenshit about heights and hadn't managed to look over the bridge to the forest around us the entire time we navigated it. I leaned forward, peeking around her shoulder, and shook my head. She had her eyes closed and felt her way over the bridge.

"You gotta check out the view, Kit."

"No thank you!"

I sighed, stepping closer, and I touched her elbow as we walked two more feet, then met the landing. "Step up, drama queen."

She went quiet then, and each instruction we received, she obeyed. But she did that with nothing more than head nods and low grunts right until the point that she was strapped to the line with a harness surrounding her. That's when the waterworks started.

"No, no! No, I can't..." She turned, grabbing for the latch to unfasten herself from the harness. I stepped forward, waving off the kid who went to help her out of the contraption that kept her fastened to the line.

"Hold on. Wait a second. You want to..." She wouldn't listen and kept a death grip on the railing, putting her forehead against the metal as she took quick, uneven breaths. "Kit..."

"I know I'm a coward. I know it. Jess was right. I'm a chicken. I know, Kane, you don't have to... But...God!" She straightened, turning her back on the landing and the stretch of forest around us as she glared at me. "This was an intensely bad idea."

"If you don't do this, you're gonna regret it."

Kit knew I was right. She understood that I was pushing, that I was only trying to help do the thing she wanted. It was written on her features—the disappointment mixed up with the fear. So, I kept pushing, hating the way her fear, her wild, manic worry, twisted up something inside my chest. I'd do any damn thing she wanted, and I knew, no matter what she said, this was the thing she wanted. This was an item she had to tick off her bucket list.

"Kane, I'm scared."

Those three words did me in. Something shifted inside my head and pushed aside the worry I had over letting Kit see anything in me that would make her think our friendship wasn't enough for me. I'd admit to myself and no one else that I felt something old and primitive for her, something I hadn't been able to shake for five years. But damn if I'd let even that get in the way of keeping her safe. More than anything, I wanted to take that fear out of her eyes.

"I got you," I told her, motioning to the kid running the zip line. "We'll go tandem."

"That'll cost extra," he tried, but I stopped his explanation with a quick glare. "Your choice, man."

And it was. I knew it. Even if there was a loud, bitchy voice in my head telling me not to get too close, telling me strapping myself to her was an epic level of dumb, I tuned it out. Kit needed me to take the worry from her, and I'd damn well do that.

But I hadn't expected her to be behind me. I hadn't expected her to wrap her legs around my waist and her arms over my chest. I damn sure didn't expect the heat from her panting mouth to move between my shoulder blades as she buried her face against my back.

"Go on three," the kid said, tapping my shoulder. He nodded at my thumbs-up and then started the countdown.

"One..."

"Kit, you gotta give me a little room to breathe here." But Kit didn't budge.

In fact, when the kid shouted, "Two," her grip got tighter and her nails sank into my chest.

"Come on, don't be a chicken..."

"Three!"

There was a small tug, and then we pushed off the landing. Kit pressed tighter against me, ankles locked, pussy warm against my back.

"Fuck," I muttered and, of course, she managed to hear that.

"What? What's wrong? What is it?" Her voice was loud, panicked, and she was breathing like she'd just run a marathon. "Kane, what's wrong?"

I couldn't admit a damn thing to her. What the hell was I supposed to say? *Oh, nothing, Kit Kat. I just like the way you feel wrapped around me, that hot little pussy of yours warming my skin?* She'd claw my eyes out.

"Nothing," I finally said. "Except you're missing all this." I slipped my hand over hers, smoothing my thumb against her skin, hoping it would calm her a little because she was missing something remarkable.

The trees sped by, shooting out a rainbow of greens and browns, like some sort of Technicolor cascade right out of a painting. The only thing that made that mad riot of colors look pale and simple was the arch of Mount Rainier straight ahead of us. We careened toward it; those peaks and streaks of white from the snowcaps were brilliant against the midday sun. All the beauty mingled with the sweet sensation of Kit wrapped around me, and I felt a little punch-drunk.

"Fuck's sake, Kit, open your damn eyes and trust that I won't let anything happen to you!"

My shouting got her attention, and I felt the slide of her cheek, then her chin against my back. The warmth from her open mouth moved up my back to my shoulder, and the vise grip on my chest went a little slack.

"Oh," she said, though I could barely make out the word. I glanced over my shoulder, squinting as I watched her profile. She looked around us, to the landscape and forest below, then to the mountain as she turned her head. She was beautiful. So fucking beautiful, and in that instant, I realized there was no way in hell I could push down what I felt for her. There'd be no gullet deep enough, no part of my brain dark enough to keep the light and color of Kit dim.

"Oh God," she said, sounding amazed. "Kane..."

The ride took minutes, maybe, but I prayed it would last forever. Being there with Kit, having her body pressed against mine, watching that awed expression over her face, how the fear left in segments, from fright to worry to dread that shifted and blinked out of her eyes. Then came the calm, the swell of wonder and a bunch of other things I wasn't poetic enough to describe. I only knew that she'd never looked more beautiful to me. Not with a shit-ton of makeup on her face or her sporting some designer gown the studio made her squeeze into that one time she'd agreed to make an appearance at the Emmys.

Right then, with Kit watching the majesty around us, I knew I loved her. And I knew, as we slowed to a stop, as she jumped and squealed when the workers released her from the harness, when she went straight at me when I got the harness off, I just knew there wasn't anyone else I wanted but Kit Carlyle.

"Kane, thank you," she said, hugging me tightly, tugging my face down between her fingers before she kissed my cheek. "Thank you so much."

Yep. I was well and truly fucked.

Lucky's was packed by the time we left the mountain. Kit hadn't taken a breath the entire time we drove back in my truck, jabbering away about the adrenaline rush and the mountain and how she thought the world "went by in a fucking whirl," as she put it.

We'd spent an hour at the bar, drinking our way through three beers each, and now Kit was on to some fruity pink drink she swore was the best thing she'd put in her mouth. It took fucking effort not to make a comment on that one.

"To the bucket list," she said, offering that pink drink toward my half-empty Guinness for yet another toast. This made the fourth one in the past two hours. "And to Jess." Kit went a little quiet then, and those hummingbird eyelashes of hers went to work. "My cousin. For pushing me to do this shit." She sipped, then seemed to think of something and pulled the glass away from her mouth. "And to you, Kane. For making me do it!"

I laughed, eyes wide as she downed the drink in one swallow. "Shit, you're drunk," I said, laughing.

Kit shrugged, dancing in her spot on her stool. "Oh, I love this song." She lifted her arms, and the hem of her shirt tugged up. I had to force my gaze around the bar, then back into my glass. "Kane, dance with me. Come on." She had one foot on the floor and the other still resting on the stool. "I love Prince. This is so much better than the Sinead O'Connor version. Come on."

I was about to say no. I didn't fucking dance, no matter who asked, but Kit stumbled, and I caught her. That low plead in her voice made me swallow back the moan that threatened to leave my mouth. And then, the asshole on the stool next to us stood, stepping to Kit's side.

"Come on, darlin'. I'll dance with you." I knew this guy. At least, I'd seen him around. The jackass had gotten drunk three weeks ago, and Crystal had thrown him out on his ass. I'd also seen him working around the bar this entire night, getting turned down by nearly every woman in the place before he settled on the stool near our side of the bar.

"The lady asked me," I told him, standing up. He didn't put up much of a fight, stepping back to look up at me before he shrugged and walked away. I took Kit's hand, ignoring how good it felt in mine, before I slammed down the rest of my beer and led her to the dance floor.

"Mmm," Kit said, the vibration of her voice moving against my chest as she rested against me. She was a good foot shorter than me and I had to lean down, but the awkward position didn't bother me.

"It's a good song," I told her, not caring if anyone except Kit could see how close I held her or how I tried to subtly inhale the scent of her hair as we danced.

"It's the best." She straightened, stretching her arms over my shoulders, eyelids heavy, smile lazy and a little ridiculous. "Prince...*he* was the best."

"Agreed," I said, watching her lashes as she blinked, amazed how they were so long that they fell to the curve of her cheeks. Her face was smooth, lineless, but there was the smallest scar along her bottom lip. I'd never been this close to her, had never once noticed that scar, but didn't want to mention it. Not when she curled closer to me, my name slurring a little when she spoke it.

"Kane." She said my name like it was something that felt good on her tongue, each syllable a tease I couldn't help loving. "Thank you, Kane." Then Kit blinked, her movements slowing, and I followed her, barely moving my feet as the song went on. I was too caught up in the way she let her tongue slide against her bottom lip, how she opened her eyes, and there was no drunken tease in the smile that shook as she watched me. "Thank you," she purred, and I stopped moving altogether, struck dumb by how slowly Kit's thumb moved against my bottom lip, how she pressed close, eyelids shutting as she whispered "Thank you" again.

And then, with the entire bar laughing and drinking around us, with my heart pounding like a drumline on play-off night, my friend Kit stretched up to her toes and pulled my face down, my mouth to hers, as she stole my breath with one long, slow, perfectly wet kiss.

Chapter Five
Kit

"**F**uck," he said as he thrust forward, sliding his long, hard cock deeper inside me. "Wanted this, wanted you for a long damn time." He filled me completely, stealing my breath as well as my ability to speak.

If I'd spent too much time thinking about what was happening, I wouldn't have been underneath Kane and about to have the most earth-shattering orgasm of my life.

"Me too," I admitted and locked my ankles behind his ass, holding his body to mine. I could've stayed like that forever. Our bodies moved together in a perfect sensual dance with no sounds other than our breathy moans and our skin slapping together.

He reared back, hovering above me and stared down with hungry eyes. "So. Fucking. Good." I wasn't sure if he was talking about sex or what this meant for our relationship.

I closed my eyes, forgetting the flurry of feelings building inside me and dug my fingernails into his skin, almost piercing the soft flesh to get at his hardness underneath.

Every muscle in my body quaked as he pummeled me time and time again. In and out. In and out. Each thrust becoming more laser focused as if he knew just the right spot to hit.

"Kit."

"Mmm-hmm," I mumbled with my eyes closed and my head tipped back, enjoying every minute of my little fantasy.

"What do you want me to do with this?"

My eyes flew open, going wide as they met the confused gaze of Dale. "Huh?" I scrambled out of my chair and ran my palm over the patch of exposed skin just above my breasts. "What?"

"This beam." He motioned with his head toward the fireplace as he swatted at the sawdust on the sleeves of his flannel shirt. "You never told me which stain you want me to use. I want to get that in place before lunch."

"Oh...*um*." My fingers worked the edge of my V-neck, fumbling with the material while I tried to get my mind from where it had been and back to where it was supposed to be. "Mahogany," I blurted out because it was the only thing I could think of after Dale caught me off guard.

He turned his head, giving me a sideways glance. "You okay?"

I gave him a big smile, totally terrified that he could read my mind and every dirty thought that had just gone through it. "Just perfect."

Dale took a step forward and lowered his head. "You sure?"

"Yeah." I wanted to ask why, but I didn't want to know if I was that easy to read. I glanced around, ready to change the subject before I said something I'd regret. "Where's Kane?"

"He stormed out of here 'bout ten minutes ago. He's grumpier than normal today. Who the hell pissed in his Wheaties?"

"You know Kane." I grabbed my design folder off the table and was ready to head for the door because I wasn't in the sharing mood, and I knew Dale would ask something else I wasn't ready to answer. "I better go find him."

"Mahogany. You sure about that?"

"Totally," I shot over my shoulder before stepping outside, leaving Dale and everyone else inside. Everyone except Kane.

His profile was unmistakable and stopped me dead in my tracks. He leaned on his truck with his hands hanging over the bed, staring at the ground and looking like he was talking to himself.

More times than I cared to admit, I replayed the moment our lips touched last night. The way he wrapped his arms around my back after I took him by surprise and held me against his rock-hard body. Time seemed to evaporate, and the music in the bar slowed along with our movements.

I never would've kissed him if it hadn't been for the alcohol that buzzed through my system and totally fucked with my common sense. Sure, I'd thought about what it would've been like to kiss Kane. He was beautiful, rugged, the right kind of man who'd make sure a woman he was with was taken care of in *every* possible way. I'd imagined Kane and me kissing, touching, at least a hundred times, but I never thought I'd actually do it.

The pink drink tipped me over the edge and stripped me of all rational comprehension. The adrenaline from the zip line hadn't worn off either, and the combination was like a one-two punch of stupid.

The way we danced, close and slow, didn't help make things clearer. Add kissing Kane to the mix, and it was the cherry on the proverbial sundae.

"Kit," he called out across the yard while I seemed to be frozen on the front porch, gawking at him like a complete weirdo. "You need me?"

I almost choked on my own spit when he asked that, but I played it off as best I could. "Nope. Good. Don't need a thing."

Kane raised an eyebrow and tilted his head because he knew my bullshit meter was off the charts. The man knew me better than anyone. Clearing my throat, I clutched the design folder tightly against my chest, trying to throw up my "Kane will not affect me" shield. "I thought we could go over the plans for this afternoon."

In typically smooth fashion, he pushed off the truck and strutted toward me like something out of a wet dream. My mouth watered as he moved toward me. His well-defined, thick arms swayed with each step, and he caught my gaze, which lingered a little longer than I anticipated.

"You okay?" he asked, standing in front of me with the same look Dale had given me.

Get your shit together, Kit.

I blinked, shaking all thoughts from my head, and managed a tight smile. "Perfect. I was just thinking about how much we still have to do to get this place ready."

"Don't worry, Kit," he said, and my eyes followed his lips, watching his tongue as it swept across his bottom lip. "I'll make shit happen."

"So..." I stalled for a moment because my mind went all kinds of places it shouldn't have gone. No matter how good it was, the kiss was a mistake, a line

I crossed that I knew neither one of us was ready for. But the pink drink...enough said. I was just about to pull the paperwork from the folder on the kitchen island when my stomach rumbled, filling the silence.

His eyes dipped, lingering on my chest for just a second before they landed on my noisy stomach. "Wanna talk about it over lunch?"

"Yes," I said quickly because soon my stomach wasn't going to be the only thing making a fool out of me.

I never had this much trouble concentrating around Kane. Years we'd worked together without issue. One kiss, the best kiss I'd ever had, but still... it only took one kiss to turn it all upside down and alter everything we were and probably would be as we moved forward.

"How about the little joint by the river?"

"Mmm," I moaned softly, and Kane's eyes dropped to my mouth just like mine did to his.

Kane's lips parted as he sucked in a quick breath, but he recovered and motioned toward his pickup. "Hop in. We'll be back before the crew's done with their lunch."

I couldn't argue. I was hungry, and the guys still had to take their lunch. It would be well over an hour before anything much got done, and I loved the little café near the river. Kane and I had eaten hundreds of meals with each other over the years. Not once had any of our meals been awkward or abnormal.

But then, we'd never kissed before either.

Kane sat across from me, leaning back in the booth as I fumbled with the silverware after we'd ordered and couldn't bring myself to look him in the eyes. "I've been thinking."

"About?"

"Well." My mouth suddenly went dry, and I couldn't say another word with my tongue practically glued to the back of my lips. Grabbing the water glass, I finally let my eyes wander to his as I gulped it down, not stopping until the contents were half gone.

He crooked an eyebrow, watching me closely, but didn't say a word. That was Kane. The strong, silent type, typically unreadable to most, but never me. But as I sat across from him, trying to avoid the conversation of last night, I couldn't think of anything else.

"Oh. My. God," a waitress said as she approached our table. Her gaze moved from me to Kane, sweeping across his upper body and soaking in every morsel of his rock-hard goodness. "Betty, it's them."

"Hey." I smiled, not unused to the attention of fans, especially in small little towns like this.

Kane's jaw tightened, but he somehow managed a tight, yet friendly smile. "How's it going?"

The woman pulled out her phone, and Betty came to stand at her side. "Look." She pointed at her screen before both moved their faces closer, getting a better look at whatever held their attention there.

I thought they wanted a photo. Kane was always a big hit with the ladies. They waited to get his attention, usually lost for words when they finally saw his impressive size in person.

"Well, day-um," Betty said, stretching the word out over a few seconds as she gazed at Kane with a smug smirk. "Looks and can kiss."

My hands flattened against the table, and my body became immobile as my heart sped up, working double time. "Um, what?" My eyes widened, gaze darting to Kane, who had the exact same deer in headlights expression I was sure spread across my features. Nothing rattled the man. Someone could've lobbed a hand grenade into the café, and he would've dropped, rolled across the floor, and launched it back through the window without even blinking, but this was something neither of us had prepared to handle.

"Jesus, that's hot," Carol, at least, that's what was printed on her name tag, said as she tapped on the tiny screen, and the music from last night filled the café.

My eyes grew wider, and the hunger in my stomach vanished, replaced by nothing more than dread. I sucked in a breath as sheer panic settled in my bones, knowing that our first-ever kiss had been filmed and shared with the world.

Kane tipped his head back and studied the women as they ogled the screen and our most intimate moment. "Ladies, mind if I see that?"

Carol flushed and didn't move for a second until Betty elbowed her in the ribs, forcing her to hand it over. Kane smiled, nodding a thank you before he looked at the phone screen, finally seeing what they had seen.

My heart was a wild mix of alarm and silence as his eyes darted between the screen and me. The face that had been unreadable moments ago was now all types of fire and fury and one I'd seen before.

"What the hell is this?"

Betty placed her hand on Carol's arm and answered the question for her. "It's Connect."

"Which is?"

"The biggest social media app in the world. People can post live videos, share their life and photos."

"So, what the hell?" Kane's loud growl caught the attention of half the café, and the entire place quieted to a whisper as they all turned their attention on us. "Someone filmed us?"

Betty nodded quickly and a little overly excited. I guessed she didn't get the pissed-off vibe Kane was throwing and the petrified one I was sporting. "Yeah. I've followed a few of the guys from your set since you hit town. Asher posted this last night, and I couldn't stop watching. I mean, look!" She leaned forward, pushing her tits a little too close to Kane's face as she pressed against the screen. "Over one million views."

"Why would someone do that?" I whispered, more asking the question to myself than anyone else. It was a total invasion of privacy and not something I'd do to even my worst enemy.

"Who the hell posted this garbage?"

"Asher," Carol answered, snatching her phone from Kane's grip with the quickness of a ninja.

Kane glanced at me, his face scrunched up because the name didn't ring a bell. But that wasn't a surprise. It took Kane more than a few weeks to learn someone's name, and even then, they had to be memorable enough for him to even bother. The man was all about respect, and you had to earn it before he cared enough to know who you were, especially a name. "Who the hell is Asher?"

"The new kid."

His eyes narrowed, his hand tightening into a white-knuckled fist. "That little..."

I shook my head, not wanting to create any more of a scene or give them anything to sell to the tabloids. Based on the number of hits to our video, the story was about to explode, but not before Kane had a chance to wrap his hands around the hipster's neck. "Ladies, can we get our food to-go?"

"Sure. I'll get your waitress." Carol jammed her phone back into her pocket. Betty stood at her side as they both gawked at us for another moment.

We smiled, both more uncomfortable than we were before we walked in, which was shocking because the silence between us was already palpable.

"Calm down," I said softly as the other customers finally went back to their food instead of the show over at our table. "Keep your shit together, Kane."

He leaned forward, pushing the water glasses out of the way with his arm. "That little fucker better run fast, because if I get my hands on him..."

"Sorry about this," Tammy, our usual waitress, said as she placed a white plastic bag on the table along with our check. "I would've said something to you about this sooner, but I figured you knew about the video."

"Jesus," Kane mumbled, his eyes locked on mine and not paying any attention to Tammy. "Has everyone seen the damn thing?"

"No," she said, laughing nervously. "Only about a million people on Connect." She paused and tapped her finger against her chin. "Then there's the couple million on Instawatch, plus anyone who's been on that online entertainment magazine. You two are all the rage right now."

"Fucking hell."

I shook my head and glared at him. "Thanks, Tammy. Sorry if we made a scene."

"Don't be silly. It's exciting to have celebrities in town, Ms. Kit. You and Kane are our favorites. We're rooting for you two." She smiled, blushing a little as she said the words. "That kiss was something else." She fanned herself, but when her eyes met Kane's, she scurried away.

"Don't act like a damn fool," I warned him as I reached into my purse and grabbed a twenty. "Just play it off. Getting pissed will only draw more attention to it."

He placed his hand on my arm, the one still on the table, and gave it a light squeeze. Lifting his ass, he pulled a twenty from his pocket and threw it on the table before I had a chance. "Looks like it's getting plenty of attention when we didn't even know the damn thing existed."

He had a point, but that didn't mean we needed to create a scene in public. I already knew that half the world was talking about us, and we didn't need to compound the problem.

We walked out of the café, half the eyes in the place following us as we left, which only made Kane angrier. I was afraid that by the time he got his hands on Asher, I'd be bailing his ass out of jail for assault and battery.

The storm was about to make landfall.

Chapter Six

Kane

The slimy, backstabbing, hipster asshole was hiding. I knew that the second I hopped out of my truck and hightailed it to the cabin. My crew was quiet, but they didn't hold back with the stares I knew must have had something to do with that fucking video.

"Where is he?" I asked Dale, kicking aside a tub of drywall mud that sat at his feet. The guy was tall but still had to stretch his neck to look at me. I could make out the small threads of worry, maybe because he knew what I'd do to that little shit when I got my hands on him, but Dale had my back. Probably why he didn't immediately let his lips loose.

"Man, what are you gonna do to that kid?"

I took a step, catching a whiff of Kit's perfume when she finally caught up to me and came into the cabin. Dale's attention went to her for half a second, then that wide gaze shot straight to my face. "You gonna tell me?" I tilted my head, not able to keep the grit from my voice. "You of all people should know about loyalty."

"Fuck that kid, Kane," Dale said, his eyes widening as though my questioning his loyalty was an insult. "I just don't want you catching shit for beating on a little punk that can't defend himself." The guy straightened his shoulders, head shaking when Kit came to my side. "Doesn't seem like a fair fight."

"It's not," I agreed.

She gripped my arm, and for half a second, I forgot what had put me in such a bad mood. But that slight touch had voices going quiet around us, as if the crew hadn't seen Kit touch me like she did just then a hundred times before. Shit, we were friends and she was female. In fact, she was a touchy-feely sort of female. Kit was affectionate to everyone.

So why the hell were they all gawking at us like we'd just come back from our honeymoon?

Without thinking about it, I glanced down at Kit's fingers wrapped around my arm then right at her face, and she got the message, stepping back to shove her hands into her pockets.

"The kid," I said to Dale, and this time, my voice went louder, not hiding the anger that had surfaced the longer I stood there waiting for an answer.

"What are you gonna..."

A quick head shake had Dale shutting up before I pointed to myself. "Fucking. Storm."

He nodded, and with that explanation, Dale's face relaxed, like he was only just remembering how I handled bullshit when it came onto my set. "Out by the trailers. Hiding. His girlfriend is an intern with the makeup crew."

I was already to the door when Kit hustled behind me, keeping her hands off me, which kind of pissed me off. That kiss last night...fuck me, it was good. It was the best, but shit, was she drunk. I figured she hadn't even remembered it or maybe she had and was embarrassed about it or just damn well wanted to never mention it again. Then those fucking waitresses had to show her the video, and by that time, I was so pissed, I clean forgot to think about what she'd meant by it. Or if she'd meant anything at all.

This was why I should have stayed clear of her. At least, with this list. Kit asked for my help, and I wanted to give it to her, but shit was it hard keeping her at a distance, especially since I now knew what she tasted like, how those perfect pink lips and soft tongue felt against my mouth.

"Fuck," I muttered, scrubbing my hands into my eyes as I stomped out of the cabin.

"Kane, come on, be rational," Kit was saying, moving at a close jog as she tried to keep time with me. "What happens if you go in there and rough up that little guy? You'll get fired and..."

"I have a contract."

The farther away we walked, the more attention we drew, but my focus was on the gray trailer near the back of the property and the noise of movement I heard going on behind those thin walls.

"Bill will find a way, you know he will. You're on his list."

"Fuck Bill's list," I told Kit, reaching the trailer just in time to hear a whisper that was no whisper at all of, "Hide in the cupboard, Asher," before Kit stepped in front of the door, holding out her arms to block me.

"Think about consequences..."

"Oh, I am," I told her, lowering her arms to move her out of the way. "Little fuckface in there needs to learn about consequences." I reached a fist over Kit's head then pounded on the door. "Hear that, asshole? The storm is here, and it's a fucking tsunami wrapped up in a typhoon."

The rustling in the trailer got faster, and I knew I caught definite shouts of "Oh, shit!" and "Run!" But then Kit touched my chest, lowering my arm with a smooth swipe of her fingers on my bicep, and I forgot for a second about the jackass inside who needed a lesson in bad fucking weather.

"Kane, please." Her voice was even, and something deep in my gut warmed me from the inside when she spoke my name like that. It was how she'd sounded last night, when my name on her lips had come out like a moan. Fuck, I'd wanted her, and for a second,

I could only watch her, thinking stupid, pointless thoughts about what it would be like to have her to myself, to remind her of how it had felt to be in my arms.

"The video was..."

"He's a kid," she said, and I swore her voice sounded like music just then. Kit had a way of working me, with a look, with a jerk of her chin, with a motherfucking sigh that got me to do things no one else could. She was doing it again, and for the life of me, I couldn't find it inside my head to give a single shit.

"Hmph." She smiled at the grunting sound but didn't move away from me. There was something buzzing between us then. At least, that's what I tried to convince myself I felt. A vibe, a buzz, a hum of energy that only sparked between two people who were connected. Like fucking magnets, we moved toward each other. Closer, breaths held, waiting and...

"Guys! There you are," Bill called, running toward us with his voice a little harried.

Fucking hated that asshole.

When he stepped to us, Kit and I backed away, me with my hands through my hair, trying to distract myself from what was probably something I made up in my own head, and her, just standing there looking like a fucking angel, all smiling and perfect and shit.

I'm pathetic.

"Listen, this whole video thing," Bill said, facing the trailer as though he didn't want anyone but Kit and me to hear what he had to say. A quick glance behind him told me he was likely giving us a heads-up before the small cluster of reporters—national, by the looks of them—made their way to us.

"The studio is eating this shit up. Whatever's going on, keep it up. They want to milk it."

"There's nothing..." I started, but Bill shook his head, interrupting me before I could explain anything.

"Doesn't matter. Since that video went live, our ratings have jumped. They want to keep up the momentum. They've had millions of new subscribers, and if we play this right, we might land a better time slot."

The reporters were noisy, their feet rustling against the leaves on the ground. I had just enough time to spare Kit a look before she plastered a wide, forced smile on her face and ran her fingers through the ends of her dark hair to straighten it before the questions started.

"Kit, can you tell us if you and Kane are an item?"

"Kane, do you think your female fans will be disappointed to discover you're off the market?"

"How long have you two been a couple?"

Between the frantic question-asking and the shuffling movement of cameras and lights, I felt the tension rising in the back of my head.

"Please, everyone, let's not jump to conclusions," Kit said, holding out her hands to bring the focus to her. Damn, she was good at this celebrity bullshit.

She glanced at me, a half smile and a wink calming me before she faced the reporters again. "There seem to be some assumptions being made that are a little... premature."

Next to her, Bill cleared his throat, and I had to fight the temptation to glare at him.

"But the video, Kit..."

"Was a lost bet," I chimed in, ignoring Bill's dumbass throat clearing. "Look at her, she's beautiful, but that shi...stuff last night was two friends making stupid bets while drinking a lot."

"So you're saying there's nothing going on?" The reporter who asked the question looked disappointed; she lowered her shoulders, and I swore I spotted a slow pout forming.

"We're saying," Kit interjected, "that Kane and I are very...close." There was a smile working over her lips that I spotted immediately as Kit's bullshit grin. She used it all the time when we played poker with the crew. The interns always lost to her. I never did, and that grin was the reason why.

"So, you're confirming..."

"She's telling you folks that it's not up for discussion," I said, exaggerating the gruffness in my voice. It was something Kit fucked with me about sometimes when the cameras were rolling. We never flirted, on air or off, but Bill liked it when I was the butt of Kit's teasing. It gave the fan sites shit to gossip about. This video sure didn't do a thing to quash that gossip.

"Okay, guys, we're filming the header install today, so we need you to head out," Bill said, waving the reporters back as Kit smiled. She turned her back to them, arms crossed as she nudged the trailer step with the tip of her boot.

"Think they bought it?" she asked, looking down, subtly glancing back to see if they were still watching. When she spotted the cameras continuing to roll, Kit squeezed my wrist, dropping it immediately as though she only just noticed they were still filming.

"Nice," I said, laughing as she feigned worry over getting caught.

"I did take acting classes at the community college."

"That explains a lot."

Kit smiled, but it didn't seem genuine to me. There wasn't the usual laughter coloring her skin, and I wondered if this was too much—the kiss she didn't remember, the faked flirtation with me

"Hey," I said, not caring who was watching when I grabbed her arm. "Anytime you wanna call bullshit on this, you say the word. I don't much like pretending for an audience, but this is your gig."

"It's yours too," she said, tilting her head to watch me.

"Nah, it's not. You know I don't like the attention." I looked toward the cabin, head shaking over the amount of work we still had to do and how that excited me. "I like working with my hands, and the network is stupid enough to pay me a lot to do that." Kit's face softened when I looked back at her. "It's a bonus that I get to hang out with my friends while I do it."

Then Kit's smile was gone, and I couldn't be sure, but something in my head told me that she hadn't liked that comment. Something I was pretty damn sure I imagined had me thinking she didn't like me calling her a friend. But why the hell would that bother her?

"Well, I guess we should get back to...what are you doing?" she asked when I gripped the door handle and swung the trailer door open. There were no exits. No back ways out, and the windows were too small for even that hipster shrimp to escape. "Kane! Where are you going?" Kit asked when I stepped inside the trailer.

I turned, grabbing the door handle to block Kit from entering. "Don't worry. I'm not going to hurt him."

"Wait!" She grabbed my elbow, eyes wide and worried before I could shut the door. "What are you going to do?"

Some of the worry left her expression when I winked at her, and I decided just then to wink at her as much as I could. The effect made my gut flutter like a virgin groom getting a lap dance at his bachelor party.

"Consequences, Kit. Consequences and some weather lessons."

Chapter Seven
Kit

"You ready?" Kane asked over the telephone as I sat on the edge of the bed, tying my shoelaces.

"As much as I'll ever be." I sighed and dropped my foot to the floor, silently cursing Jess for adding the marathon to her list.

I'd always been physically fit, but only to a point. I never had to try too hard and never went to the gym because my line of work helped keep my muscles toned and my weight in check. Being on an active construction site, there was always something that needed moving or doing.

"If you want to do the half marathon, you have to train for it. You can't just wing this kind of shit."

Kane was suddenly in his military mode. All gung ho for the day's activities. The man lived and breathed exercise and discipline. His background made it necessary for him to have a clear path, which often led to his laser focus.

"Don't you think we should do this after work?"

"Stop stalling. I'll be there in five. Be ready," he said before the line went dead.

I tumbled backward onto the mattress and groaned. The man was impossible. Yesterday, when he went after Asher, I almost had a full-blown panic attack. When Kane pulled him out of the makeup trailer, I thought for sure he was going to knock Asher out, consequences be damned. But being Kane, therefore unpredictable, he did something I never would've thought about doing. He shaved the damn kid's waxed and curled mustache. Asher begged for forgiveness as Kane threw him into the makeup chair, holding him down with one arm, and grabbed the clippers from the counter. When Kane turned them on, Asher began to shriek in terror with his eyes growing wider the closer the clippers came to his face. I didn't think I'd ever seen a more satisfying grin on Kane's face than I did as when he ran the clippers over Asher's trembling lip.

"Consequences," Kane mumbled before tossing the clippers back on the counter and finally releasing a very pale and petrified Asher.

I couldn't stop my mouth from hanging open as I watched the entire scene. I guessed it was better than him coldcocking a kid who was less than half his size. Kane's punch could've damn near killed the skinny thing who probably hadn't been hit a day in his life.

CHELLE BLISS & EDEN BUTLER

The sound of Kane laying on the horn less than five minutes later had me scrambling out the door. "I'm coming," I yelled, but he couldn't hear me over the country music that poured out the windows of his beat-up pickup truck. He watched me as I jogged in his direction, his arm slung over the back of the seat, completely unreadable and totally Kane. I slid across the seat but didn't lean back because his arm was still there, and I wasn't sure what else to do except slam the door. "Feel better about yourself today?"

"I do."

"The kid is probably devastated."

"He'll survive. He's lucky I only cut off his mustache." He smirked and laughed roughly. "Damage could've been far worse."

"Ain't that the truth," I muttered and rolled down the window because suddenly being this close to Kane in such a confined space made it hard to breathe. "Where are we going?"

He tipped his head forward, and my eyes followed, landing on the giant mountain that sat behind my temporary housing. The top towered over everything in the city, and from a distance it was beautiful, but that didn't mean I wanted to go anywhere near it. I was more of a "appreciate beauty from afar" type of girl. Never had I endured any type of strenuous physical activity unless it involved work, and even then, I tried not to work up a sweat.

"That's too big, Kane. I said a marathon, not a triathlon."

"Conquer the mountain, and the marathon will be child's play."

I blinked, gawking at him like he had two heads. "I wanted to go for a short jog, not a backbreaking hike."

Kane shook his head. "Never wants to work up a sweat."

"I sweat," I argued, crossing my arms over my chest and staring out the window as we headed toward the mountain.

Kane thought he knew everything about me, but he didn't. There were times, although few and far between, where I didn't mind a little sweat or getting dirty. Those moments usually involved very few clothes and typically another person, but never a mountain and tennis shoes.

"Uh-huh."

As he pulled on to the highway, we passed no less than five media trucks parked at the nearby café. Cameras, reporters, and bystanders filled the tiny parking lot.

"What the..." I whispered.

"I took care of them."

I turned to Kane and blinked a few times, momentarily speechless. *He took care of them.* "What did you do?"

He looked at me, his gaze sweeping across my face as he shrugged like what he'd said wasn't terrifying. "I took care of them."

I clenched my jaw and narrowed my gaze, trying not to lose my shit. "You said that. What does that mean, Kane?"

"They were camped outside your place. I told them to wait at the café, and we'd try to give them an exclusive later."

"You what?"

"They're bastards. They would've hounded you. So, I took care of it."

The one thing Kane hated more than hipsters was the media. He hated any big event the network planned which required our attendance. America clamored for more Kane Kaino, the hottest handyman on television. But he didn't want anything to do with it, usually staying right at my side or standing in a dark corner, brooding away from the media spotlight.

"We're giving them an interview?"

"Nope." His tone was clipped as he wrapped his fingers tighter around the steering wheel and adjusted himself in his seat. "But it worked."

Bill was going to be pissed Kane had tricked the media. There was no doubt they'd show up on the set again, and Bill would do everything he could to accommodate them. He, along with the studio, loved that we were in the spotlight, even if it was an invasion of our privacy.

Resting my forehead in my hand, I closed my eyes and exhaled, long and slow, barely able to keep my anger in check. "Why would you do that?"

"You want them following us?"

"No."

"Well."

"You lied to them."

"I said 'try.' I didn't promise anything. That's why we're going to the mountain. If you jog on these roads, small town that it is, the reporters will follow. You want that?"

I grumbled under my breath, hating that he was right even if he was wrong. "No."

"That's why we're going to the mountain. I lured them away to give us some privacy."

The color on my thumbnail came off in flakes when I chewed on the tip, prying away the already chipped polish. Kane and I hadn't spoken about the kiss, the video, or the repercussions. "Do you want to talk about what happened?"

"Kit, listen. What happened is in the past. You were drunk, and we've been friends far too long to let it become an issue."

I bit down, practically ripping the entire top half of my nail clean off as soon as he said the word *issue*. The alcohol gave me the courage, lost in the moment, to actually kiss Kane, but in no way did it diminish what I'd felt as our lips touched. I'd thought the kiss meant something to him, but clearly, I was the only one who felt anything.

I'd watched the video at least a hundred times, studying every second of the footage and reading through the comments. Kane looked all in. At first, I think I'd surprised him, but then he wrapped his arms around me and seemed to enjoy himself.

I'd be lying if I said I never thought about things moving forward between us. He was good and honest, loyal, and even if he was just my friend, he *was* attractive. But he'd always spoken about relationships like they weren't for him. His privacy was important to him, but even his mother had told me once, at a Fourth of July barbecue, that Kane never seemed interested in anything but looking after his family. Mrs. Kaino had been disappointed by both her sons. She'd sworn she'd never get to be a granny the way Kane and Kiel acted with women.

So I didn't give too much thought to making a move or hoping for things that probably wouldn't happen. Still, that kiss...maybe my eyes deceived me, but I thought after all these years, I could read his body language when he wasn't putting up a front.

"Yeah. It's not an *issue* for me if it's not for you," I said, ignoring the knot in my stomach and playing it off like it was a drunken mistake.

Shit.

Kane and I were coworkers and, just as he said, friends. We'd been that for years. Hearing him say those words shouldn't have hurt as much as it did, and I was afraid of what that meant.

When he finally parked, he turned off the truck, sliding sideways on the seat and staring at my profile.

I kept my face forward along with my eyes because I didn't want Kane to see the hurt I was feeling.

"Look at me," he grunted.

Slowly, I turned my face and wiped every bit of emotion right off it, just like I'd seen him do a million times. "Yeah?"

"Lay it out."

"What?"

"Lay. It. Out."

I clenched my hands together, trying to keep the scream that was creeping up my throat down deep because I didn't feel like getting into an argument right now. The day was already going to be long, and to have us both pissed off wouldn't do us any good.

"I got nothing," I told him.

"I call bullshit."

"Kane," I said in a supersweet voice. "You can call it whatever you want, but there's nothing to lay out. We walking, or we going to keep sitting here, talking like you got a pussy too?"

My words must've hit a cord because his body rocked backward as his eyes widened. "You got a lot of shit to sling today, Kit. I'll give ya that. We're walking."

"Thank fuck," I whispered and reached for the door handle, but Kane stayed put in his seat. I climbed out and, with my still unreadable face, held my arms out in the air. "You coming?"

He stared at me for a few seconds before he followed, jumping out of his truck and coming to the back, meeting me before I could walk away. "Look at you. All fired up."

I raised my chin, refusing to admit the obvious. "I ain't fired up."

"Scorchin', babe." He smiled.

I rolled my eyes, stepping to the side and out of his way. My face might have been unreadable, but my body threw me right under the bus.

Twenty minutes ago, I couldn't imagine climbing to the top of the mountain, but after the conversation we'd just had, I hoped he could keep up. "Just try to keep up, old man."

He grunted, following close on my heels as I pushed aside a wayward branch and stepped foot on the trail. I paused for a second, craning my neck to see the top, but it was too high to see much of anything besides the treetops. Kane used the opportunity to move me aside, wrapping his hands around my upper arms before lifting me in the air and setting me behind him, to take the lead. "Follow," he said, barking at me like I was his lap dog.

I growled. He glared over his shoulder, throwing me a warning before he took a step forward. "Too much bad shit up here. Let me move everything out of the way. We can't have you getting hurt. Bill would have my balls."

I didn't want to tell him that I wanted his balls too. I shook my head. That didn't sound right, even in my head. I mean, I was pretty sure he had nice balls with just the right amount of weight to them, but that wasn't what I was talking about. I didn't want to touch them, making him crazy with lust, did I? I laughed. The internal war inside my head was getting a little out of control, and Kane noticed.

"What's so funny?" He lifted a log that had fallen over the path, throwing it into the brush instead of stepping over it like most people would do.

"Nothing," I said and bit down on my bottom lip to stifle my laughter.

Kane moved on, dropping his line of questioning as we made our way up the path. When going upward and looking straight ahead, only Kane's very fine and muscular ass filled my field of vision. Less than a mile in, he stopped, and I almost smacked his two cheeks with my face.

"It's so damn muggy." With his back to me, he grabbed the hem of his T-shirt, lifting the material over his head in one quick motion.

Fuck.

I'd seen the man shirtless a hundred times over the years, but suddenly I couldn't look at him the same. Each muscle in his back rippled, moving in perfect synchronization. My mouth watered, and the thin sheen of perspiration that had dotted my skin started to grow, feeling every bit of heat he was throwing.

"You okay?"

I raised my eyes, meeting his as he glanced over his shoulder. "I'm fine," I managed to say through my harsh breaths, the climb and his bare chest making it impossible for me to get enough air.

"We're moving."

I stepped forward, not looking where I was walking, and started to tumble. Kane turned quickly, grabbing me near the waist, and kept me upright. My hands flattened on his biceps as they flexed under my weight. My eyes darted to his, my fingers digging into his skin, and I sucked in a breath, both in shock that we were touching each other again and that I almost took a header because my damn foot got caught under a tree root.

"I gotcha."

"Thanks," I said, my face way too close because the only thing I could smell was Kane. The mountain seemed to disappear, the wildlife scattered, and only we existed in that moment, perched on the side of the mountain.

He peered down at me, and I gazed up at him. Neither of us spoke a word, barely moving as our hands stayed on the other's body. For just a second, he let that unreadable face go, and I saw the man staring at me like he wanted to sink his teeth into me. I'd seen that look before during the hundred times I'd watched the video of us.

Kane could insist that the kiss meant nothing to him, but after I fell into his arms, I knew there was more than friendship between us. It was written all over his face. It was an awful idea. Kane and I were friends and coworkers. Neither of us wanted to ruin what we had going, but I think we were way beyond the point of no return.

"Kane," I said, finally coming to my senses and unwilling to make the first move again. I wanted to, though. God, how I wanted to kiss the man again, but there was no way in hell I'd be initiating anything.

"Yeah?" he replied, his hands tightening around my waist.

"You going to hold me all day, or are we hiking?"

He cleared his throat and dropped his hands from my sides, the unreadable look firmly back in place. "Hiking."

When he quickly turned and I had the view of his fine ass and chiseled back again, I did a little celebratory dance. I knew I wasn't the only one who felt that tingle from the kiss the other night.

Chapter Eight

Kane

I never got what I wanted. Not really. As a kid, sometimes what I wanted got put on the back burner because there were three of us and Kiel or my mother needed something more. Braces or medicine or a new car, that shit came first, and I always made sure I came last. But I was no damn martyr. The things that I could have, the things my mom or brother didn't need, were the things I took for myself. The last can of soda in the fridge because my mom had heart palps and didn't need the caffeine. Kiel, well, he never took care of his teeth until he was a teenager, and the soda would have wrecked them even worse. And girls— sometimes my stupid little brother let his dick get him into trouble. I took it upon myself to get him out of it. So I stole the girls I knew he was feeling because he was stupid about females and didn't realize when the opportunists were coming for him. Girls who thought he could give them babies and a free ride, or girls who would make Kiel work his ass off for nothing more than to spend all his hard-earned money on them.

I shut that shit down for his own good, and as I sat across from Kit, listening to the forest around us as we cooled off from our hike, I realized it might be best if I shut down this nonsense about the bucket list. Well. At least the items she'd avoided discussing with me.

"So," she said, twirling the water around in her half-empty bottle. "There's something I've been meaning to talk to you about."

"Yeah?" My heart went off a little, beating like a drum because what I'd avoided talking to her about, the thing I knew we'd eventually have to discuss, was right here in front of me.

"Yes," she said, staring down at her feet. "It's just... Jess was funny about things. I mean, about me and things..."

"What kinds of things?" Fuck me, I was teasing the siren, and that bitch was hungry for my soul. I knew better than to play dumb with Kit. I'd avoided the topic of the last few items on the list because I did my level best to avoid the idea of Kit and sex. Love wasn't on the table. Not for us. It couldn't be.

She downed the rest of the water, rolling the bottle between her palms as she went on avoiding my stare. "She...Jess thought I hadn't ever really had...good, um, sex."

Shit. There it was all clear and present: the flash of Kit lying on her back, looking bored, unsatisfied as some faceless asshole kissed her full breasts, then lower. I might have imagined her yawning, before the daydream shifted and I barreled through the door, kicking out the hapless jackass, and fell on top of her.

I exhaled, now the one ignoring her gaze as I poured what remained of my water onto my sweaty hair. When I opened my eyes again, Kit watched me, her face unreadable like it had been just a couple hours ago in my truck. Damn if this woman wasn't good at keeping whatever she thought off her face.

"All right," I finally said, careful not to ask her to elaborate. That daydream needed not to be in my head, not while we were alone in the woods, sweaty and, I had to admit, feeling the adrenaline of the hike running through me. Would have been the perfect time to show Kit what good sex was like.

Shit, man. Shut the fuck up.

"Well, we haven't discussed it, but Jess added good sex to the list." She sounded nervous, like there was something stuck in her throat that she couldn't dislodge. "You read the list, so you know..."

"Well, I do, but hell, there are other things too. Like the president thing and the whales. Even the kiss could come before..."

"We did the kiss," she said, her words coming out in a rush, as though she couldn't believe I hadn't remembered.

"That wasn't..." My heart was throbbing now, inching up like a flight-or-fight sensation into my throat. "She said you were to have a toe-curling..."

"Moan-worthy, ruin me for all other men kiss." She nodded, moving a small smile on her lips. "Yeah. That one got checked off the night after we zip-lined."

If I were a different man, if Kit weren't my friend at all, I'd have gotten up, dropped to my knees in front of her, and shown her how much better my kisses were when they were planned. But her confession did something to me. I hadn't felt the swirl of excitement in the pit of my gut since I was a kid getting his first glimpse of tits. Kit sat across from me on a small boulder, blinking all innocently like she was real and honest and not trying to bullshit me.

There was sunlight glinting off the dark color in her hair and in her eyes. Her full lips looked dew-kissed from the water she'd just drunk, and the lines of her beautiful body were glistening with sweat. I'd never found her hotter than I did right then.

"Well," I started, clearing my throat to make myself sound impassive and not like the giddy asshole I felt. "I guess I should say thank you."

Kit shrugged, her smile wavering as I leaned forward, elbows on my knees. She pulled her long braid over her shoulder, messing with the end like she needed something to do with her hands out of nervousness, maybe some self-conscious habit she had that made her seem indifferent.

"So," she continued, seeming uninterested in talking about the compliment she'd just given me, "the other item... The...well, the sex."

"You offering me something?" I couldn't help asking that smartass question with a laugh so she knew I wasn't serious. "I mean, if the kiss fucked up shit for us, God knows what sex would do."

Kit didn't laugh. She looked, in fact, mildly disappointed in my joke, and I wondered as I pulled the smile from my features, if there *was* something she wanted to lay out to me, even though she'd sworn there wasn't. But the look on her face stopped me from throwing out any other asshole comment. There was real worry on her face, mixed with a little disappointment that I was sure I invented.

"Hey," I started, holding up a hand to get her attention.

"No, you're right." Kit sat up, dropping her empty bottle to the ground to move it between her feet. "You and I...well, that's probably not going to work for a lot of reasons, but I have to admit Jess was right." Kit inhaled, closing her eyes like she needed a second to steel herself before she nodded, looking me squarely in the eyes.

"I *have* had a lot of really bad sex. It would be nice to change that. But, I suppose that's something I'm going to have to figure out with...someone else."

It felt like some fuse got lit inside my head. Then came more daydreams, more quick flashes where Kit was on that bed, naked this time, touching her tits, moaning like she couldn't help herself, like she was so turned on and her pussy was begging to be touched. But it wasn't me there helping her out. It wasn't me kissing her, tasting her. That faceless asshole was back and was a fucking god of sex. At least, the noises Daydream Kit made seemed to tell me that.

I clenched my jaw, the quick surge of fury working through my veins like some jealous asshole who'd just been told his woman didn't want him anymore. Couldn't be helped. And even when I grunted a response and stood, picking up the protein bar wrappers and empty bottles of water, stuffing them in my backpack just to keep from saying any damn thing to her, I couldn't quite manage to keep myself calm.

"Kane?" she said, her voice sounding worried, maybe a little curious.

"We need to head back down. You won't have any breaks in the marathon, and we only have about two hours of daylight left."

"Are you okay..."

"Fine." Even I didn't believe me, not with how biting and sharp my tone was. "Let's just..." I let out a breath, trying to keep the tremble from my hands. "Let's just head out, all right?"

"Yeah," Kit said, but her inflection was dry, a little insulted.

There was no way around it. I'd have to settle for pissing her off and do my best not to fucking think of the asshole who'd be in Kit's bed. Whoever he was, I fucking hated him already.

I was an asshole. And a prick. And a jealous jackass who'd made my best friend feel like nothing. At least, that's what I thought, and I was pretty sure Kit thought the same thing. It had been a couple of days since that hike in the mountains, and I'd ended the day dropping her off at her place, not saying much because I couldn't get past the unwarranted anger I felt at Kit wanting to fuck someone who wasn't me. Even though I knew that would be a bad idea. Sex with her would be bad, not because we'd be bad together, but because it would be good. It would be fucking fantastic. Too good. Too much. Impossible to forget.

I couldn't let that happen. I couldn't wreck the good stuff we had together.

"I'll see you on Monday," I'd told her when I dropped her off, frowning when she just jumped out of my truck and went into her small rental without even a backward glance. I'd waited for it, even idled in front of her place five minutes after she'd gone inside, but she hadn't bothered to look out the window or text me later when I was home alone nursing a beer. No "What the fuck is wrong with you?" text or "You get whatever is up your ass out?" Nothing. Nada.

So, I did the only thing I could do that night. The same thing I'd done when I got home from Lucky's the night we kissed on the dance floor. I slid back in my king-sized bed, slipped my hand under my shorts, grabbed my cock, and thought about Kit's sweet lips and sweeter ass.

But that hadn't made things better, and two days into our workweek, Kit still seemed irritated with me. I had to do something to make her think I wasn't an asshole. I mean, she knew I was an asshole, but not to her. Not usually. The perfect opportunity came when that fuckface Bill spotted Kit and me standing a good five feet away, not acknowledging each other as we both listened to Dave, our director, talk about the segment we were about to shoot.

"So, Kit, you're going to explain why you wanted the fireplace resurfaced. Don't forget to mention the broken mortar." Dave moved his palms up, thumbs touching to make a mock lens as he nodded for Kit to stand next to the reconstructed fireplace surround. "We'll start with you next to the edge, then you can walk to the front of the hearth, and that's where Kane will be."

The man nodded me over, and I took my position on one knee, holding up the river rock from the floor. Kit had ordered the stone from a company out in Gatlinburg, and we'd only started the rebuild two days ago.

"Kane, when she comes to your side, relax, answer her questions, and remember not to give too much detail. I want this conversational and..."

"Flirty," Bill said, standing behind Dave. The

director's attention went to his producer, and the guy frowned, shoulders lowering as Bill continued. "We've discussed this," he told Dave, waving the man off when he groaned. "Kit, when you walk to Kane's side, stand real close, maybe touch his arm a little."

"Why?" she asked, folding her arms as though she needed somewhere to keep her hands so she wouldn't tackle the man.

"The video, remember? The studio will expect..."

"That's stupid," she said, her irritation surfacing when Bill frowned at her. It wasn't often Kit let anything get to her, but today seemed not to be the day to ruffle her. Bill was too damn stupid to realize that.

"It's not stupid," he told Kit, her glare firm as she stepped up to him. "Look, if the studio wants..."

"Hold up," I told him, moving in front of Kit. "Give us a minute, and then we'll be ready to film." I glanced at Dave, jerking my chin at him when the director shrugged, already uninterested in playing up the Kit and Kane flirt fest. To Bill, I cocked up an eyebrow, challenging him with one shift in my expression to pester her again.

"So fucking stupid," Kit said when Bill and Dave left us alone. She turned to face the fireplace, kicking one of the loosened stones in the hearth. "I didn't sign up to do this shit to play up the reality show drama."

"I know that," I said, leaning against the wall as I watched her. "But, you know, more attention might mean more exposure."

Kit jerked her gaze to me, her frown tight. "You hate the attention."

I nodded, scratching the scruff on my chin. "But you don't, and what have you always told me? You'd do just about anything to get popular enough to sell your own stuff. This," I said, motioning to the crew and cameras behind us. "This is a bullshit hurdle, and you know it. Means to an end. You want that little shop in Seattle to sell stuff you design. How many drunk confessions have I heard you making about that shop in the past five years?"

"And you just wanna build furniture and burn your logo into the underside of each piece."

It was true. Kit and I, we weren't the celebrity types. We wanted to be comfortable, not rich. We wanted to be our own bosses, not run empires. We wanted simple lives that didn't involve drama. But none of that would come to us if we didn't work for it, and right now, that meant smiling for the cameras and maybe fanning the flirting flames.

"I do," I told her, moving closer to her. For a second, I forgot about the show and the monkey act Bill wanted us to perform. Just then, I only thought about how I could reach out to her, pull her forward, and Kit would fit perfectly right under my chin. She'd rest against me, cheek on my chest, and I'd thread my fingers through her hair. It would take less than ten seconds, and she'd be there. All I had to do was reach out.

"We ready, guys?" Dave asked, his smile forced.

"Yeah," Kit told him, pausing to hold my arm. "I'm sorry about..."

"Hell no," I told her, squeezing her fingers back. "That was all me. I, uh, guess I'm a little territorial about you."

Kit held her breath, her eyes widening as she watched. "Why?"

One step and I could reach her. I could bend down and kiss her, give Bill something that would make the studio wet themselves. She had the fullest bottom lip and smelled like honeysuckle.

I blinked, laughing low to disregard the look she gave me right then. "Hell, Kit, truth is, I'd act that way about anyone you'd want to bring in to help you with your list. I mean, shit, you remember when that jackass contractor came in to help on the lake house two summers ago?"

"I do," she said, her head shaking, and I relaxed when she laughed. "I thought you were gonna kill him when he asked if I wanted him to install the beams."

I scratched my chin again, relaxing at how easy Kit's smile was. "See? Territorial." The lighting guy adjusted the bulbs as the makeup girl came in to touch up our faces. "We'll do this and give Bill something that will keep him quiet for a while."

"Oh?" Kit said, letting the girl fix her lipstick as she focused her attention on my face. "What did you have in mind?"

"Nothing too drastic." I bent down, letting the wardrobe guy straighten my collar. "But I can do charming. Passable flirting."

"Okay," she said, taking her place on the mark next to the fireplace. "Let's see what you got."

Shit, I wish she hadn't said that. I could flirt with her. I could charm millions of random fans who hoped for some sort of hookup between Kit and me. But deep down, when the cameras were off and the lights were dimmed, what I really wanted was to show Kit exactly what I had and how I thought it was all hers.

Dave yelled "Action," and we rolled with it. Kit smiled at the camera, a lazy, sweet look that made her seem approachable, real. It was one of the things I liked best about her. She was beautiful, anyone with a pulse and good taste could see that, but she wasn't made-up or too pretty to be approached. That smile was welcoming, it was genuine, and I guessed that's what had made her so popular.

"The hearth was dated, and the brick around the fireplace surround needed something fresh." She took two steps and stopped at the mark next to me before she nodded. "Speaking of fresh things, Kane, tell me about the stone you used for the fireplace."

"River rock from Tennessee," I started, my grin set because I knew she liked it. Had told me so a half a dozen times. "This ain't some fancy quarry stone either, Kit."

"No?" she asked, taking a half step back when I stood, handing her the stone sample.

"No, ma'am." She examined it, then tossed it in the air, and I caught it. "This is one hundred percent Smoky Mountain rock, specifically harvested from Three Forks near Elkmont in Tennessee. We like to use products from the South, as you know." I tilted my head and moved that smile from grin to smirk. "Prettiest things in the world come from the South."

"Is that right?" Her smile widened, and I knew she got where I was headed.

"Yep." I leaned closer, tossing the stone back to her. "You're from the South, right, Ms. Kit?"

The blush was present, coloring her face, and I laughed right along with the crew as her smile went wide and she nudged me in the ribs.

"Well," she said, grabbing the stone out of my hand. "We'll finish up the fireplace today and then start on the staircase. But first, y'all have to excuse me. There's an awful lot of BS muddying up the room, and I need to change my boots."

"Perfect," Bill said when Dave cut the shot, and I laughed to myself, watching Kit as she walked away, thinking to myself that, for once, Bill was right.

She *was* perfect.

Chapter Nine
Kit

"Why are we here again?" I pushed the overgrown branches aside, following Kane up what seemed like an endless trail.

He glanced over his shoulder and cocked an eyebrow. "Bucket list," he grunted before he turned around and marched forward up the mountain.

The man had been in a sour mood since we finished taping. Bill had dubbed the episode "The Big Flirt." Kane stayed true to his word, almost knocking me off-kilter a time or two with his innuendo and damn good flirtation. But as soon as the cameras turned off, something inside him shifted, and the flirty, fun Kane disappeared.

Lifting my backpack higher, I tried to keep up with Kane, but his crankiness had started to wear on me. "We could've just pitched a tent behind my rental house."

"The list said *in the mountains,* Kit, not near one."

He had a point, but I wasn't really into the experience. Between the bugs, the uphill climb, and the thought of sleeping under the stars next to a grumpy Kane, I wasn't exactly looking forward to the next twelve hours of my life.

Kane came to a quick stop, and I face-planted into his gear, bouncing off him like a ping-pong ball. I started to topple over when he reached back, grabbing me before the weight of my pack pulled me down the trail. "Jesus, woman," he muttered, still holding the loop at the top of my pack.

I batted his hand away. "You should give a girl some warning before you stop like that, Kane. I could've died."

I was being overly dramatic, but if I tumbled down the mountain with the pack strapped to my back in an endless free fall, I would've ended up in the ER. Reporters would've swarmed us, and I could already see the headlines in the gossip magazines.

A hint of a smile flashed across his face as he stared down at me and dropped his hand near his side. "I'd never let anything happen to you. You know me better than that."

I thought I knew everything there was to know about Kane Kaino, but the last week showed me the exact opposite.

"This looks like a good spot."

"We're done climbing, then?" I pulled the pack off my back and dropped it to the ground, thankful the hard part was finally over. "Because I'm ready to pass out."

"A little physical activity is good for the soul," Kane said, setting his pack, which was twice as big as mine, near his feet.

I couldn't take my gaze off him as he stripped off his shirt and tucked the scrap in his back pocket, something I'd seen him do a million times with very little effect. Maybe it was the way the sunlight streamed through the trees, bouncing off his taut and rock-hard abs that held my attention, but whatever caused the trance, I knew nothing good could come of it. Kane didn't seem to notice; he bent down, his shoulders now glistening as he started to dig through his backpack.

"While you collect firewood, I'll set up camp."

"Uh-huh." I didn't move, but somehow, I found enough common sense to form a few syllables, though not much else.

The kiss, the drunken one at the bar, had replayed in my head a million times since it happened. My body pressed against his solid and massive chest as I touched my lips to his soft, lush mouth. A bare-chested Kane kneeling before me hadn't made the visions stop either, but amplified them.

"Kit," he said. "Firewood."

I blinked, my feet still frozen to the ground and my gaze glued to his naked flesh. "Yeah," I whispered and blinked again.

"You okay?"

I nodded and pushed away the thought of Kane's soft, wet lips pressing against mine as his arms settled near my waist. "I'm fine." I cleared my throat, twisting my body to the side to break eye contact with his bare flesh. "Get a freaking grip," I whispered to myself, and Kane didn't seem to notice.

"It's going to get cold tonight. We'll need a fire to keep warm."

"Right. I'll handle the wood." I grimaced as soon as the words were out of my mouth. The small phrase sounded way more sexual than I expected, and Kane didn't miss a beat.

Bent over his pack, Kane glanced upward with a cocked eyebrow. "Yeah?"

I ground my teeth together, annoyed I'd suddenly become a bumbling idiot around him. I stalked off toward the woods across the clearing, trying to put as much distance between myself and the half-naked Kane as I possibly could. For what felt like the hundredth time, I had to remind myself that Kane and I would never happen. Kane wasn't feeling me like that, and I supposed he never would. But damn, what a fucking view he gave me.

"On it," I called out with one hand in the air, unable to face him and thankful for a little break.

We consumed almost an entire bottle of Jack Daniel's as the cold of night started nipping at our skin. The stars sparkled above our heads, dotting the colorless sky as the fire crackled near our feet. The time had passed quickly between prepping our camp for the night and making dinner. The mountain was peaceful, yet loud with the riot of wildlife moving around us, hidden in the deep brush but making their presence known.

"Kane."

"Yeah, Kit?"

"Do you think there's something after this?"

Since Jess had died, I hadn't been able to think of much else. Besides whatever was happening between Kane and me, I thought about what happened to us after we left this place. Is our life only a small part of our journey, or after our eyes close for the very last time, is it infinite blackness, much like the sky above our heads?

"After the mountain?"

Turning my face toward him, I rolled my eyes and smacked his side. He knew exactly what I meant, but Kane never liked to get too heavy, and we'd avoided all discussion of my cousin's death besides the list. "I'm being serious now."

He rubbed his fingers against his forehead and faced me. "I don't know, Kit. I wish I had all the answers for ya."

"What if there's nothing afterward?"

The very thought was paralyzing. I never claimed to be a holy roller, but the possibility of something more, something bigger, had made dealing with loss easier somehow.

"Then you won't know any different." His hand covered mine, giving my fingers a light squeeze. "There's no point in fearing the inevitable and pondering what we aren't meant to understand."

"It's not that easy."

Men seemed to have an easier time with death and the unknown. Maybe they were genetically coded that way. I let fear rule me, sometimes paralyzing me from doing what I wanted because I was too chickenshit of the consequences.

"Don't let fear rule you," he said, seeming to read my thoughts. I hated when he did that. Kinda loved it too. "That road is a bad one to travel. It'll suck you up. Consume you entirely if you let it. Concentrate on what's in front of you and shut everything else out."

I laced my fingers with his, tethering myself to what was in front of me or, in this case, at my side. I rolled over and propped myself up on my elbow. "It's hard to shut everything else out when I have this list hanging over my head."

His gaze didn't leave mine as he remained flat on his back, one arm tucked under his head. "We're working on the list, Kit. Soon you'll be done and can focus on something else."

"Are you going to help me with everything?"

He sat up, breaking our connection, and stared down at me. "I'll help you with what I can. The kiss, though. I don't..."

"Shh," I said, pushing myself upward. "The kiss is done. So, hush."

His eyes flashed with confusion or maybe it was recognition, but I clearly saw the change. "It's done?"

"We talked about this, remember? The bar. The other night? Music. Dancing. The kiss," I reminded him and scooted closer, our knees touching.

"You were serious about that?"

"Yeah. I told you I was."

"But the list said ..."

"Uh-huh," I whispered and set my hand on his leg as the Jack Daniel's coursing through my system made everything seem easier. My head was fuzzy; my inhibitions were gone. Kane had promised to help with the list. He'd read it. I knew he had. It was the kiss and likely the sex part that had him nervous and initially refusing to be my wingman. Now, though, there had been the zip-lining and him helping me prep for the marathon. We'd spent the past month getting up at the crack of dawn to run. He'd helped me streamline my diet, and he hadn't pulled away when I kissed him that night at Lucky's.

The kiss in question was everything my cousin said it should be, and I hadn't been able to get it out of my head since the moment our mouths disconnected.

Maybe it was the Jack. Maybe it was the memory of the kiss and what it told me I could expect if Kane ever agreed to make a move, but something switched off in my head just then. Something that was old and hungry and told me to take what I wanted. I forgot all the warnings I'd given myself about Kane and me being together. I even forgot the convincing I'd always done to remind myself that we would never be anything but friends because, in that moment, I didn't think about him as my friend. Right then, Kane was a man. A man I wanted.

"I don't think..." His voice trailed off when my hand slid up the inside of his leg. "What are you doing, Kit?"

"I thought we could...you know." I waggled my eyebrows, feeling a bit frisky and totally carefree. "Make this a two-for-one deal."

Kane rocked backward, shocked by my words. "Two for one?"

"Yeah."

He tensed, his eyes going wide, but Kane didn't stop me when I inched closer. He didn't do much but stare, looking amazed as I brought my face right next to his.

"It's...on the list," I said, grazing my fingernails along his neck. He smelled like heat and fire and a scent that was all Kane. It made my mouth water and my body convulse.

"What…" Kane let me straddle him, even leaned back, his eyes still wide but focused as I wobbled on top of him. "*This* is on this list?"

"This…" I said, scooting so close that my pussy grazed his dick. "This is leading up to what's on the list. Or, at least, it could be." Kane froze just then, his eyebrows coming up as though it was the only move his shock would let him make. I took advantage, loving the coarse feel of his fingertips against my arm when I leaned over him and the sweet heat that crept out of his opened mouth. "Figured you were so good at the kissing, maybe you could show me…" The smallest touch of my thighs against his, the tease of my tongue along his bottom lip, and Kane shut his eyes tight. "Show me what good sex is like."

He released a strangled noise, then stopped me, fingers closing around my biceps as he sat up. "Fuck's sake, Kit, you've got no clue what you're saying."

"Oh, I know." I wiggled over him, feeling drunker and a hell of a lot pleased when Kane's cock jerked against my leg. "And you do too."

It took Kane three deep inhales and the twist of his head away from me as though he needed not to see my expression before he sat up straight, loosening his grip on my arms.

"The thing is, how I am when I'm alone with a woman ain't the sweet, well-mannered Kane you know."

"Oh shit." I laughed, my head dipping back as a wave of humor overtook me. "Then I feel sorry for every woman you've taken to bed." He didn't smile, and I rolled my eyes, not undone in the least by his frown. "Give me a break, will you? You're an asshole to everyone but me."

"Granted," Kane said, moving his fingers off my arms to rest on my hips as though the movement were an afterthought. As though he didn't realize what that relaxed, comfortable gesture did to me. I bit my lip, holding back a comment of how close we still were and how his cock hadn't softened in the least. I might be drunk and feeling a little reckless, but Kane was turned on, and holy hell was I impressed.

"But," he said, blinking when I wetted my bottom lip, "when I'm with a woman, alone with a woman, I tend to take control. It's...it's the only way I can..." He cleared his throat, moving his hand as if he wanted to drop the explanation.

"The only way you can get off?" When he nodded, I relaxed my shoulders, suddenly more aroused than I'd been seconds before. "So unless you're bossing someone around, making them serve you..."

"No." There was no hesitation in his tone. Kane, in fact, sounded more serious than I'd ever heard him before. "Don't get it twisted, Kit. I give. I give until I'm weak and weary, but me, with a woman...in my bed..." He paused, and I could have sworn his dark eyes had turned to coal. Something warm and burning twisted my insides, and just then I was sorry I sat so close to him, that I was this close and couldn't move at all. Damn, I wanted to.

"It has to be the way I want it." Kane shifted, leaning back on his palms as I watched him. "I'm not gentle, Kit. I'm generous, but I'm not gentle."

I was pretty sure my panties had just melted right off my body.

"Oh," I said, my face warming as Kane watched me. There was something in his expression I couldn't place. Something I wasn't sure I'd welcome if I ever saw it again. Kane's mouth was wide, his lips full, made for kissing. Made for sin, and God help me, the fear he kindled inside me just describing what it would be like with him had me walking a line I wasn't sure I could cross. Wasn't sure I could make myself turn away from it either.

"Umm," Kane said, tapping my hip once to get me to move, and he stood, offering me a hand to help me stand. "So, maybe you want to rethink the sex stuff. Maybe you should conquer the other items first."

"Maybe," I said, dusting off my shorts as I sat back down in front of the fire.

The forest had gotten quiet, and my repressed fear of nature and all things animal that weren't big Samoan carpenters who helped me zip-line down the side of a mountain resurfaced.

"Here," Kane told me, handing me a thermos. "It's coffee. It'll take the piss and wind out of your blood, so you won't feel compelled to..." He waved his own mug between us, and I caught his meaning.

Jump my bones. That's what he meant, but Kane being Kane, he wouldn't call me on it. He'd wait for the perfect moment, likely when I was feeling myself too much or a little too proud about something I'd done. Then, he'd not too politely reminded me of how handsy I'd been here on the mountain.

At the moment, I didn't care about his teasing me. I was still reliving his "I'm generous, but I'm not gentle" confession and trying like hell to keep my libido in check.

He sat across from me, staring into his mug, and I tried to drown out the noises of the forest around us. There were animals calling to each other—nature and instinct coming together to breathe life and survival into the next season. Sex. Lots of it all around us. Creatures doing the thing that was the most natural to them.

When a particularly loud shriek echoed through the forest and I jerked so quickly I dropped my thermos, Kane watched the woods, eyes sharp, focused until a slow-moving grin tweaked his bottom lip.

"Mountain lions," he provided, then seemed to regret the guess as I released a low gasp. "Don't worry. They aren't hungry. They're.... courtin'."

"They're fucking?"

"Can't you tell?" He nodded behind me, when a shriek clapped against the trees like a streak of lightning. "Call of the wild."

"I wouldn't know."

There was a little too much whine in my tone just then, and I tried my best to ignore Kane's frown or how he looked for all the world like he felt sorry he hadn't let me have my way with him. But I didn't need the pity. If I was honest, as the coffee worked its magic and my solid buzz got less solid, I realized that jumping Kane out in the middle of the forest probably wasn't the best idea.

I wouldn't force myself on someone who didn't want me, no matter how drunk I was.

"Listen," I started, my gaze shooting to his face, when he started to speak at the same time.

"Kit..."

Kane held up his hand, telling me with one gesture that he needed to speak. "You're beautiful. You're smart. You're funny, and it sucks that your cousin left this at your feet." I leaned back against a tree trunk as Kane crossed around the fire and sat at my side. The wood smoke was almost as comforting as the warmth that spread through my body when Kane sat next to me.

"You're...my friend." I hated how the word sounded in his dry tone, but I managed to keep my expression neutral.

"Truth is, you're the one person I don't mind being around at any given time of the day." Kane leaned forward, folding his fingers together as he rested his arms on his knees. "Most people get on my nerves."

"Not Kiel."

His shoulders moved when he laughed. "*Especially* Kiel."

It was a lost cause. I knew that. Kane dropped the wrong F-word, and it sobered me right up. That sweet smile of his also loosened any hold I had on the notion that I could somehow get him alone and naked. Drunk logic never worked right.

"Well, I'm sorry if I got all...handsy."

Kane scrubbed his fingers through his hair, sighing as he rubbed the back of his neck. "Hell, Kit, I'm not saying you didn't turn me on."

"Well, I know that."

He nodded, waving a hand as the only gesture of defeat he'd allow me. "You being my friend and all, and being drunk, again, and we're all alone out here." Kane leaned back, releasing a small groan as he stretched out his long legs and rested against the tree trunk. "I might not be gentle in the bedroom, but I'm not an asshole either."

It made sense, Kane's reasoning, even if I didn't like hearing it. He was real and genuine and so fucking gorgeous, sometimes looking at him left me a little dumb. But he was right. The kiss had made things a little sideways for us. Being with him? Out here in the wild? I wouldn't put it past Bill to set up cameras between the tree limbs. Besides, even if I wanted Kane, I didn't want him drunk.

He exhaled again and curled his arms over his chest. I could see the subtle lines of the veins in his thick arms, and the muscles of his forearms were pronounced and so damn tempting. But it did no good to go on watching and wanting him. Not when it would lead me nowhere good.

Still, there was an item I needed to tick off my list, and if Kane weren't up to the task, I'd have to find someone who was. When I'd mentioned sex and me with anyone other than Kane on our hike up the mountain, he'd gone all frosty and weird on me, and I didn't know why. It was just sex. Nothing serious. Nothing all that personal, really.

"Kane?" I said, staring at the fire in front of me as it cracked and popped against the darkness around us. He offered me a sleepy grunt in reply, and I pulled up my knees, circling them with my arms. "If you don't want to help me with the sex thing...do you know, maybe know someone who would?"

"What?" The downed leaves under him rustled when he sat up, jerking to attention like I'd just gut-punched him. Kane rubbed his eyes, his head tilted toward me. "Do I know..."

"Maybe Dale? He's single, right? He still dating that girl from Tacoma?" I turned, facing Kane as he gawked at me. "Or maybe, who was that guy who used to hang out with you back in Seattle? The rugby guy from New Zealand?" I went through the list of men I could recall Kane had mentioned knowing or the guys I'd seen him hanging out with in the city or around Lucky's on the weekends.

They'd all been handsome, like Kane, though not quite as brooding and sexy. But the only other person I knew would even come close to my friend was the one person he'd likely never want me to be with. Even if it was for the purposes of the list. Still, how different could they be?

"Hang on," I said, the handsome face popping to the front of my mind so quickly that I didn't notice Kane's expression or how wide his eyes had gotten. "You said Kiel's single now." I finally turned toward him, smiling, though his expression still didn't register. "Do you think he would want to..."

"Hell fucking no!" Kane said, his voice growing so loud that the shrieking sounds of animal sexy time behind us went quiet.

"What the hell is wrong with you?" I asked, finally paying attention to his face, catching the snarl on his top lip and the tightened muscles around his eyes. "Kane..."

"Not Dale. Not my friends. And for damn certain not my brother. Not now. Not ever."

"But you said..."

He stood, stomping to the tent to zip back the opening. "It's late and I'm tired and I'm pretty damn sure you're still drunk. Time to hit the sleeping bags."

"But, Kane..."

"I'll take this one," he said, nodding toward the second tent across the lowering fire. Kane waited for me to stand, still holding open the door to my tent. He went on waiting, not saying a word, not letting that scowl leave his face until I gave up the fight, the drink and argument and almost sex that was never going to happen all weighing down on me in the few seconds it took for me to stand next to him and shimmy inside the small canvas tent.

Outside my sealed door, I could just make out Kane's low grumbles, words that were too angry, too muted for me to hear clearly, and in the distance, the quiet refrain of some animal somewhere, doing what came naturally to him.

Lucky bastard.

Chapter Ten
Kane

I blew out my knee junior year tackling a wiry sophomore who was trying to impress the Patriots' scout. Northwestern and our NCAA division, I guessed, were minor league for this guy, and he wanted out. Asshole had some sort of scheme working with his offensive lineman; arranged to take me out if I got too close to him post-pass and the two-hundred-forty-pound lineman swiped my legs out from under me and sent me off the field permanently.

I never knew what happened to the lineman or the first-round pick. Hadn't heard anything about either of them since I got pulled off the field on a medic golf cart and spent three months in PT telling myself my football career wasn't over.

It took my mother's convincing and Kiel landing a prime spot at NYU to make me realize there were bigger needs in our family than my shot at glory on the gridiron. I'd returned to Seattle, back to my mother's modest cottage, and started the long road to recovery. It was then that my job as Kiel's overseer kicked into overdrive. Mom got sick, couldn't work much, and Kiel was too damn smart, too damn slick, to do much more than hit the books. If he wanted to keep his scholarships and his place at NYU, he couldn't slack. I made damn sure of that.

Eventually, I finished college, after Kiel graduated from NYU and Mom's diabetes got manageable.

But for all the big brothering I'd done, there were lines I wouldn't let him cross. Lines he was inching toward right fucking now on my set.

Standing too damn close to Kit.

"Kit Kat got herself a new man?" Asher's laugh died on his tongue the second I glared down at him. He swallowed, and the sound of his throat working was almost funny. *Almost.* The hipster blinked at me, the pale spot where his stupid mustache had been still lighter than the rest of his face. "What...what did I..."

Dale shut him up, slapping the kid on the shoulder. "Dude, why are you always poking the storm?" He nodded toward Gin and the small crew of landscapers that had set up a line to lay pavers along the cabin walkway. "Go be useful and stop annoying Kane."

But my attention wasn't on the scramble the hipster made toward Gin and her crew of laborers.

She shot a look at Dale that was half smile, half glare and I shook my head when the man bristled.

I returned my focus to my kid brother and the smooth, practiced smile he shot down at Kit. I knew the look. Hell, I'd invented it and gave Kiel lessons in how to perfect it.

"Kiel rarely shows on set," Dale said, coming to my side. His focus shifted to my brother, then back at me, but my gaze was locked on Kit, laughing as Kiel twisted a stray peony petal at her, offering her the flower as an afterthought. "Kane?"

"Hmm." It was more noise than answer, and Dale must have heard something that worried him in my low grunt. He stepped in front of me, blocking my view.

"So, what I see here is you, glaring at your kid brother because he's making moon eyes at Kit."

Attention jerking back to Dale, I couldn't keep it there for long. "The fuck are you talking about?"

Kiel shouldn't be standing so damn close to her.

"Uh-huh. Yeah, I'm the one that's out of my head." That asshole laughed, shooting a glance over his shoulder before he moved again, arms folded as he stood close enough that I had no view at all of anything but his ugly face. "Fuck's sake, man, when are you gonna make a move?"

"With who?"

Dale rolled his eyes, smile lowering. "Jesus, you've been all alpha male around Kit since I got here, likely before that time. I'm telling you, do something or quit beating on your chest when anything with a dick gets near her. It's embarrassing."

Dale was out of his head—and a huge hypocrite. Gin walked in front of us, barking orders to the hipster, and Dale's gaze followed her like a puppy whining over his mama.

Yeah, but *he* thought *I* was embarrassing. I was about to point out that he hadn't made the move he clearly wanted to. But just then, Kit laughed at whatever dumb shit Kiel fed her, and she brushed a hand against his arm and let it stay there, and any excuses or insults I thought of yelling at Dale got squashed as I headed for my kid brother.

"You said Kiel's single now," she'd said, *"Do you think he would want to..."*

No, I silently answered her. *Not Kiel, not fucking anyone.*

It made no sense for me to be jealous. It made no sense for me to do the chest-thumping thing Dale had accused me of, I knew that shit. But just Kit mentioning being with Kiel, asking him to take her, her asking anyone to do the same... Fuck me, I couldn't take the image. It was too much.

Once, I'd caught Kiel's ass moving up and down as he fucked Tiffany Williams in the back of our mom's gardening shed. He'd been sixteen and, from the looks of it, clueless as to what he was doing. As I moved across the set, steps heavy, gravel crunching beneath my feet, I couldn't help but still see his skinny ass, jerking up and down, this time, moving over Kit and... *fuck*. Something snapped in my head. I took two more steps, came to my kid brother's side, and pushed his shoulder.

"Kane..." he started, but he tensed at my hand on his chest, then frowned when he lost his balance and had to catch himself on the porch railing.

"What the fuck?" he asked, righting himself to square off in front of me.

"You got a job here?" I asked him, cheek twitching as I narrowed my eyes at him. "Huh? There something I can do for you?"

"Kane," Kit tried, but Kiel talked over her.

"Damn, big brother, see if I stop by to see your ass again." He adjusted his coat, stretching his neck and inhaling, catching hold of the easy calm that was never too far from his reach. "Bad day?"

"We're busy," I told him, sounding lame. We were never too busy for visitors. Hell, Kiel had been on set so much that he knew the crew by name.

My brother looked over my shoulder, to the crew that were breaking for lunch, to the others that were in between jobs and having smokes before he looked back at Kit, then at me. "Yeah," he said, smiling that smooth asshole smile of his. "I can see you're slammed today."

"Kane," Kit started, pushing on my arm. "You're being rude."

Kiel echoed her, exaggerating a frown that I guessed was supposed to express his offense. Total bullshit. "Very rude." He dusted off his sleeve as though he weren't sure how he'd recover from the made-up insult he felt. "Now, you can apologize."

"Kiel," I said on a sigh.

"Yeah?"

"Go fuck yourself."

I said it through a growl. There wasn't any humor in my tone, no mocking smile on my face because I'd meant it. Kiel was invading my space. He was getting too close to my...to Kit. Was I a jealous prick? Yep, probably, but for half a second it felt good to see the surprise washing over my kid brother's face. Half a second longer and I spotted Kit's frown, that soft pout that moved across her mouth and the barely there line that dented between her eyebrows. I hated that it was me putting that look on her pretty face.

I didn't explain. I didn't apologize. Instead, I turned away from my brother and the worried look on Kit's face and left the set before I did something I wouldn't be able to take back.

Chapter Eleven
Kit

"**W**ant another?" Kiel asked as he tapped the empty beer bottle in front of me.

I gazed at his thick finger, and my mind filled with all kinds of dirty thoughts. Hot, naked Kiel. Wide chest brimming with muscles, hovering over me with those to-die-for bedroom eyes peering down at me. "Sure."

I knew I should've left a long time ago, but when Kiel showed up at Lucky's, I thought maybe it was meant to be. When he invited me to stay for a drink, I figured, why not? Kane wasn't even willing to discuss helping me with the sex bit on my list, and I figured his brother would be the perfect substitute.

Still, he *was* a substitute. Not the real deal.

"Two beers and two vodka shots," Kiel told the bartender before tossing me a smirk. That look reminded me of another tempting grin, and the man attached to it. The Kaino men swam in a delicious gene pool. Both were all male, all rugged, and striking. They were alphas—strong, disciplined, and so damn fine.

But where Kane was all hard edges and gruff passion, Kiel was smooth contours and sweet words. He was seduction personified in a fit, designer package.

I wasn't sure which turned me on more. At the moment, Kiel was taking the lead.

As soon as the bartender placed the drinks on the bar, Kiel pushed the beer and shot in front of me.

Another grin that he hid behind his shot and I mimicked Kiel, shooting back the vodka, trying not to think of the last time I'd done shots. With Kane. Beautiful Kane and the night I kissed him.

I chased the shot with my beer and tightened my eyes closed, trying to block out the memory. Kane *was* unbelievably sexy. Women basically threw themselves at him and begged for his attention. Kiel was no different. Just a younger carbon copy of his older brother, one a little more carefree and easygoing, which was nice for a change.

"So, what has my brother's panties in a wad?"

"How 'bout another shot?" I mumbled, motioning to the bartender. He placed two more vodka shots in front of us, and I grabbed mine before Kiel could even answer me. Explaining this to Kiel would either work to my advantage or blow up in my face entirely.

Just as the glass touched my lips, Kiel tipped his shot in my direction and smiled. The man wasn't in a hurry to do anything, even drink. I wanted the buzz I already had to deepen and make the bullshit from the day melt away. Watching him, I held my beer between us and waited for his words of wisdom.

"May all your ups and downs be under the covers," Kiel said and tapped his glass against mine.

I choked out a laugh, still managing to get another swig of beer down my throat. Without thinking, I watched the slow movement of his tongue against his bottom lip, and I held my breath, momentarily forgetting about anything at all but that mouth, that tongue, and where it could be put to good use.

Thoughts of Kiel naked, his fine, hard ass moving up and down as he pumped into me swarmed my mind.

Wipe it away, Kit.

Kiel's tongue darted out again, swiping the remnants of the drink off his full lips as my head started to buzz, making it impossible for me not to think about him sexually.

"So, my brother..."

It took me a second to refocus but the mention of "brother" and the reminder of the last time I'd been in this bar eradicated that small fantasy of Kiel that had just begun.

I sighed, leaning against the bar. "He's impossible," I muttered. I didn't even know if that word was big enough to describe the clusterfuck going on between Kane and me.

I hated that this stirring, this thing deep inside me, was resurfacing. I'd made it go away before, that night I saw Kane standing in the breezeway of the banquet hall the network had rented for our Christmas party. We'd only met a few weeks before and had already become friends. The attraction had been brewing since the day I'd met him, but I was sure it was all one-sided.

He'd been honest, but not to me.

"What do I think of you and Kit?" he'd asked Bill, frowning when the producer offered him a cigarette he didn't take.

"Yeah. She's fine, right? Think I can hit it?" Bill had been drunk and a little sloppy. Kane, though, looked sober, and I watched him in the reflection of the glass in the lobby window. They could see me standing near the doorway, and the second I heard my name, I'd stopped, wondering what my new coworkers would say about me. I'd been a little more than curious, especially to hear what Kane thought.

"No," Kane told Bill, turning to glare down at the man. "You definitely can't hit *it*. She's out of your fucking league."

"But not yours?" Bill had asked, his face screwed up in a sneer. "Think you're better than me?"

"Fuck, I know I am, man. But, Kit? No way. *We* couldn't touch her. Not any asshole in this building. And I suggest you don't try. I damn sure won't."

Despite his promise, I couldn't help but fall a little bit for Kane that night. He was protective, even back then. He was fiercely loyal, and I'd wanted him, all of him. But it wasn't going to happen. Not when he promised he'd never try.

Still, it took me months to push back what I felt, until that desire became a pulse and not an electric current. After his rejection in the mountains, I realized Kane was sticking to his promise.

"He giving you shit? He was in a particularly assholeish mood today."

I plucked at the label on my beer, tearing the paper away at the top edge and glanced at Kiel. "You know about my cousin, right?"

"Yeah." He turned, caging my body in with his knees, one arm propped on the bar and the other holding his beer against his leg. "Sorry about that, Kit."

I couldn't hide my sadness, and I didn't even bother around Kiel. Besides Kane, he was the only person I knew who wouldn't judge me for not being the perky and always happy Kit Carlyle. "When she passed, she left me a list."

"A list?" he said, but the half smile told me he might already know about Jess's list.

"A bucket list filled with things I've always been afraid to do."

"You're fearless, Kit." He smiled easily, bumping my leg with his knee. "What makes you quake?"

"Silly things."

"Nothing's silly."

"You haven't seen my list, Kiel. Kane's helped me with a few things, but..." I took a sip of my beer, avoiding eye contact with Kiel because I wasn't sure I could get the words out of my mouth without sounding like a horny, sexless idiot.

Kiel's chest puffed out, and his back straightened. "My brother's a chickenshit. I'll do what he won't."

Typical brothers, those two. A few months after meeting Kane, then his brother, I'd caught on to the huge competition that was always between them. I had male friends from school with brothers as a kid. Boys always had this unspoken competition with each other. The Kaino brothers were no different. They never spoke about it, but I guessed growing up in the shadow of a brother like Kane couldn't have been easy, not even for Kiel.

"But you don't know what I have to do." I shook my head when he only shrugged like nothing on Jess's list should warrant worry. I picked one of the hardest examples just to get that grin off his handsome face. "I have to shake hands with a president."

Kiel's eyebrows drew down, and his lips flattened. He probably wasn't expecting anything as big as meeting the present or even a former commander in chief to make my list of things to do before I died, but I could thank Jess for that one.

"Well..." He paused, his teeth working on his bottom lip. Damn, it was plump, and from the looks of it, velvety smooth skin that was made for kissing. "Luckily, I have a buddy who's on the president's detail." He elaborated when I could only manage to gawk at him. "I should say, the former president. You know he's coming to Seattle, right?"

I sat up straighter, my stomach fluttering. I *loved* the former president. He was my hero, and I'd spent an entire month on the phone trying to land a seat at the fund raiser he was speaking at in Seattle. I'd had zero luck.

"Kiel...are you serious?" I asked him, holding my breath.

"Yeah, I could probably swing a meeting somehow."

My eyes widened, and I couldn't help the shake that had taken over my fingers. "No way!"

He nodded slowly, a lazy smile planted firmly on his face. "That fund raiser is packed, but I could work some magic."

"That would be amazing." Somehow, I knew Jess would approve. She was far more political than I was, but she swore I was a secret fangirl.

"I'll ask around tomorrow. See if I can call in a favor."

I practically jumped onto his lap and wrapped my arms around him. "Thank you. Oh my God, thank you," I whispered against the warm, silky skin of his neck.

Kiel turned his face, and the scent of his cologne hit me. It was different from what I'd always picked up on Kane. Kiel's scent was refined, expensive, and I couldn't help how it worked up something inside me that felt a lot like lust. When I leaned back, trying to put space between us, Kiel tilted his head, bringing our lips so close I felt his breath skid across my mouth.

"Anything for you, Kit. Anything," he whispered, shooting a slow, sexy look at my face, to my mouth, and up again right at my eyes.

Damn, he was good.

Slowly, I peeled my body away from his, my arms suddenly cold at the loss of contact. Kiel Kaino's pull was undeniable and just as strong as his brother's. Both lured me closer and sucked me in with little effort.

"You're the best."

"I meant what I said." Kiel reached a hand up, grazing the tip of one finger over my cheek. "Anything you need, Kit, I'm your man." He smiled, that perfect, white, panty-dropping Kaino smile.

His touch was soft, smooth, just like the slip of his gaze when he went on watching me, taking a second to stare before he cleared his throat and sat back, elbow again on the bar. "So...what else is on this list?"

"Um." I turned my body forward and my gaze away from Kiel. God, this was so embarrassing. Kane knew about my lackluster sex life. There was very little we didn't know about each other, but Kiel...he was a different story. He wasn't my best friend. He never had been. I loved him because of his brother, but in all the years I'd known him, I'd never once thought about sleeping with him...until now. "Most things we've already finished."

"Like?"

"We went zip-lining, and we've been training for a marathon." I tore another piece of the label away from the bottle, rolling the scrap into a ball between my fingers, and finally glanced at Kiel.

"What else? And don't bullshit me." That grin returned, and for some reason, the gesture had me believing I couldn't lie to him. Kiel cocked an eyebrow, staring at me like he expected nothing but the truth. "I know my brother doesn't lose his shit unless..." His eyes widened as the pieces must've clicked into place. Placing his beer on top of the bar, he lifted his ass and pulled his stool closer to me. "You got the list?"

I nodded, and he motioned for me to hand it over. Rummaging through my purse, I pulled out the folded paper and handed it to him. It was easier for me to let him experience the list for himself than to say the words out loud. Somehow, the humiliation didn't seem so great if I didn't actually *talk* about it. That's where Kane and I were alike. We didn't need to speak much in order to communicate. We were on the same playing field, using our actions more than syllables, at least when it came to each other.

Kiel's gaze moved across the paper as he rubbed his chin with one hand, running his thumb across the bottom corner of his lip. His eyebrows shot up just as I'd expected when he must have reached the one item that had Kane in a tizzy. A moment later, he folded it up, following the embedded lines and slid the paper back across the bar.

He was all confidence, a total professional as though what he was about to say was some sort of rational arrangement and not an act that would make that Kaino competition look like *Monday Night RAW*.

"I'll do it," he said quickly without so much as a hesitation in his voice. "If he won't man up, I can fill his shoes."

"But, Kiel..."

He placed his finger against my lips for a moment. "Shh, you're in need, and I'm the perfect choice to help."

Being needy was the understatement of the century. With the amount of work piled on my shoulders, I honestly couldn't remember the last time I had sex...at least, amazing sex, because lackluster fucking was typically my norm. "I really shouldn't just sleep with anyone."

"Who said anything about sleeping, Kit?" He raised an eyebrow and smirked, stealing my breath once again.

"Well." I couldn't speak, and in all honesty, could barely think. In my head, this had seemed like a good idea, but now, with Kiel sitting next to me, offering me a roll in the sack, I wasn't as confident about ticking that particular item off the list.

But then a flash of memory came over me—Kane's soft mouth, his strong, demanding hands...and then, him pushing me off his lap as we camped in the mountains.

Damn.

I wanted a warm mouth and big hands. I wanted my body rocked and my pussy buzzing. I wanted all that with Kane, but it was clear to me now that he wasn't willing to help me out.

I glanced at Kiel, returning the smile he gave me, and swallowed down the doubt, wiping it from my system. This was about the list and my cousin. It was about putting the past to bed and looking toward the future. It was about being greedy and wanting to be swept away. Kane wouldn't give me that. Kiel would.

"The only thing I can't help you with is falling in love because I'm not the right man to fill those shoes." Kiel shrugged, waving a hand in forced apology. Then he looked around, moving closer, and I leaned in too. "But I can fuck ya silly and make you forget your name for a little while."

I ignored the brush of heat that colored my cheeks and offered him a smile, hoping he bought the indifference I tried to pull off with my shrug. "I'm not looking for love, Kiel."

I already loved someone and it wasn't Kiel, but with no hope of anything more happening between us, I could at least get lost in one Kaino and get one step closer to finishing the list and having my life return to normal.

"Then, I'm your man."

Chapter Twelve
Kane

There were three sounds I couldn't stomach hearing. One was a siren, loud and screeching, sounding like a panicked scream, announcing to the crowded city streets there was a shit-ton of trouble. That was never a sound that set well with me because it never led anywhere good. Second to that was a baby's cry, especially one who can't be consoled. It's the wailing shriek of pain, something that doesn't disappear until you walk away or they pass out. That one I didn't like because it filled me with a helpless, useless sensation, something I never wanted to be.

But, the worst sound I think I'd ever heard was the desperate cry a woman made when she was scared, when she was so devastated that nothing that sounded anything at all like clear words left her mouth.

That was the sound that rattled through the receiver when my phone rang. My heart skipped beats, and I held my breath the second I heard Kit's high-pitched, "Kane, I need you."

The fact that she needed me because my fucking asshole of a brother had let her down had me pressing my foot harder against the accelerator as I sped toward Seattle.

"It's stupid, crying like this," she'd said, doing that sniffle thing she did when she was trying to hide the fact that she was upset. It reminded me of the same crack in her words that came after she'd gotten the call that Jess had died. "I just...when I heard the president was speaking today, and Kiel promised to get me in..." She paused, sniffling again before her words came out disjointed and breathy. "Jess...she knew I'd always wanted to meet him...just shake his hand."

I'd listened to each wobbling word as I'd moved around my rental, half dressing, half listening as I tried to keep my own voice calm.

"It's not stupid," I'd promised her, silently listing the ways I'd do bodily harm to my kid brother. With each passing second, that list got longer and more brutal. The bastard had fucked up big-time, and I wasn't about to let that shit go.

"He said he'd do you a favor, and he flaked." I'd taken a breath, holding the cell to my ear as I tore through my closet looking for something suitable to wear. It was a speech but not formal, so no suit, I didn't guess. In fact, I should have just settled on jeans and a T-shirt. But the second Kit explained, in that shattered, sniffling tone of hers, that Kiel had landed press passes to hear the former president's speech at the Westin Hotel in Seattle, that he'd even managed to find out when the perfectly timed speech would end and where the greeting line would be as the man left the building, I'd decided I had to finish the job.

"Besides," I'd told her, sliding on a pair of black Dickies and a gray button-up, "the man is your idol. Shit, how many times did you have me helping you register voters or toting boxes of bumper stickers in my truck for you to pass out every time he ran for president?" That earned me a pleased sigh, and some of my panic ebbed but not one fucking ounce of my anger. As I slammed my front door closed and hopped in my truck, speeding through Ashford to hit the freeway, I added "two swollen eyes" and "a split bottom lip" to the list of things Kiel needed done to him.

"Kane... Look, the other day on set with your brother..."

She didn't finish, likely thought my loud exhale was me gearing up to say something. Instead, I cleared my throat, figuring I should explain why I'd acted like a jealous boyfriend, but I chickened out, asking her for the second time in ten minutes where she was. "Near the kitchens?" I'd asked, breathing a little easier when she spoke and her voice sounded clearer.

"They won't let me any farther without a press pass." I could make out her heels clicking against what sounded like a tile floor as she walked, and I had to push back the image of Kit's long, forever stretching legs in a skirt and tall heels.

I shifted in my seat, blinking when something came to me. "Ah, the Westin, you said?"

"Yeah."

I nodded, though I knew she couldn't see me, but I smiled, remembering a guy I knew from an old construction job we both had with the city fifteen years back. "I'll be there in a bit. Leave everything to me. I know somebody who can get us in."

"Right here." Chris Lewis nodded toward the crowd, pointing out three empty chairs at the closest table by the kitchens. "That table is sold, but I know for a fact Senator Collins is on the fifth floor getting personal lap dances from two Little Darlings' strippers."

"Nice," Kit said. The smile lit up her face, even I could make that out despite the lack of lighting around the banquet hall.

There were at least two hundred round tables in the hall, all draped with white linen tablecloths and simple centerpieces. The president hadn't been announced, but his wife was on the stage, looking like something out of a pinup movie, her dark skin lineless, beautiful as she stood in a cream dress that accentuated her curves, surrounded by the dark burgundy drapes of fabric that covered the windows behind her on the stage.

"He won't show?" I asked Chris, pulling Kit back when she looked like she might want to make a beeline for the empty seats. "Wait till she finishes. We can sneak in when they stand and clap."

"He won't show," Chris told me, shaking my hand when I offered it. "I'll make sure he stays distracted. It's good to see you doing so well, man." The guy shifted his gaze from me to Kit, then smiled when he watched me again. "Long overdue."

I didn't bother correcting him, half wondering if Kit had heard the implication behind Chris's words over the first lady's speech. But Kit's focus was on the stage, and her eyes widened, making her look mesmerized the longer the woman spoke.

"Thanks, Chris," I said. "I owe you one."

"No, you don't." He held up his left hand, and his smile went wide. "Fourteen years next month, all because my wife thought you were too grumpy."

I laughed, feeling a little nostalgic over the memory of the worst blind date of my life. Bethany Wilkes hadn't liked me one bit, and she might have left me in that restaurant when I'd clammed up and didn't give much away. Hell, I'd only agreed to the blind date to get my mother off my back about me not dating anyone. But Bethany had been a good Samoan girl, someone my mom thought would be perfect for me. She was pretty enough. Had a banging body, but there was zero spark.

Well, there was zero spark until I ran into Chris outside the restaurant, and he and Bethany started up a conversation as I went to grab my truck. I stood zero chance with her after that first introduction.

"Glad I could help you out, man."

"Likewise," Chris said, nodding to Kit then me before he walked toward the back of the hall.

Just then, the first lady announced her husband, and we took advantage of the crowd's roaring claps and standing ovation as the overhead spotlight landed on the former president who bent to kiss his wife and shake hands with the governor.

I led Kit to the empty table, guiding her with my hand on the small of her back. The noise of the crowd died down, and we sat next to each other, our attention on the man at center stage. He was tall and thin, looked a lot older than I'd expected, though I guessed he was probably more rested, and a lot more relaxed now that his second term had ended.

"He's amazing," Kit said. There was no hint of upset left in her tone, no sniffling wail that had greeted me two hours ago when I picked up my cell. The second I'd spotted her in the hotel, she'd run to me, face against my chest, fingers curled around my collar like I was the lifeline she'd been waiting for.

Gotta admit, that shit felt good. No matter that I'd made an ass of myself just a couple days ago on the set because Kiel had stood too close to her. Like always, Kit got over my mood and attitude like it had never made an appearance. Like always, I'd forgotten everything but making sure she was taken care of, that she wasn't upset, because that's what I did best. That's who we were—friends, sure, but more than that. We were each other's people. We had each other's backs. No amount of pissy attitudes would change that shit.

She was right about one thing. The man on the stage was amazing. He was impressive, and while I'd never been in his fan club the way Kit had, I respected him. He was charming, articulate, and as far as I could tell since I didn't really pay too much attention to politics, meant what he said when he said it.

The speech progressed, with the president cracking jokes, earning laughs and rounds of applause here and there, but my attention wasn't on the intelligent man trying to drum up votes for his party's local senatorial candidate. I gave exactly one shit about politics and it wasn't a very big one, but I loved watching Kit's expression. It was open, awed. The tears had dried off her face, and the slow wobble in her chin was completely gone now. Every now and then, she'd look away from the stage, shooting a glance at the side of the stage or the exits, I guessed trying to see if anyone was coming to kick us out. But then she'd look at me, eyes soft, expression relaxed, and I stopped caring about what the president had to say or how many laughs his corny jokes got.

Kit looked beautiful, as always, but there was something so open, so exposed to the look in her eyes as she listened to the speech. Those large dark eyes were wide, unblinking, and her lips were separated slightly open, enough that I could just make out the tip of her pink tongue when she wetted her bottom lip.

Shit, I wanted to kiss her. No matter what I'd told her about wanting her the way I did or how it had to be for me. Just then, I didn't think about keeping Kit at a distance. I didn't think about her list or the things I definitely wanted to do to her but couldn't subject her to. In that second, I only knew she was happy, she was amazed, and she had never been more beautiful to me.

"That's why I think it's essential that we elect folks who will assure that the next generation..."

"He's wrapping up," Kit whispered, leaning next to me so close that I could smell the hint of coffee on her breath. She took my hand, moving one side of her mouth up as she watched me. "Even if I didn't get to shake his hand, this is enough. Kane, you did this. You made this happen, and I don't know what I'd do if you weren't..."

"Come on," I told her, cutting her off when the crowd stood again, and the president waved to the crowd, his wife at his side.

"Kane...wait, we can't..."

"Jess said shake his hand, not just hear him speak." Kit kept up with me as I pulled her through the crowd, spotted two of the men Chris had talked to to get us past security and through the employee hallway.

"But, Kane, there is no way..."

"You giving up?" I asked her, shooting a frown over my shoulder. That stopped her, and Kit tilted her head, moving a slow smile over her mouth. "Didn't think so."

We made it to within five feet of the stage, bypassing the gathering crowd of reporters as they congregated toward the backstage area, near a roped-off section that led from the stage to the back entrance. There were no velvet ropes or plastic tape sectioning off the area. But there was a row of men, all decked out in black suits and white shirts, black ties, dark shades; all with earpieces as they stood shoulder to shoulder, attention on the grouping of reporters and the small crowd of hotel staff that inched over each other, getting up on their toes to see past the Secret Service.

"Damn." I heard Kit say, holding on to my arm as we stopped behind the reporters. She followed as I moved, leaning to the right to see what we could make out in the smallest space between the stage steps and the first Secret Service man. I pulled Kit in front of me, but I could easily see over her head as we both angled our bodies toward that opening.

I was about to apologize to her, feeling shitty that I hadn't been able to make up entirely for Kiel being such an asshole. I'd even gone so far as to lean down, closing my eyes against the smell of her hair and the heat of her skin. But then there was a small commotion from the reporters, and the security team inched to the left as the governor left the stage, then several more people, and Kit gasped, pointing to the steps as the first lady descended.

"Look, Kane..." she started, and I nodded, smiling at the excitement in her voice.

"Kit, I'm sorry I couldn't..."

"Ms. Carlyle?" We heard, both of us looking up when a mammoth Secret Service man stepped away from the crowd and stood right in front of Kit.

"Yes?" she said, stretching her neck to look up at the guy.

"Someone would like to speak to you." He paused, glancing up at me. "Both you and Mr. Kaino."

"Oh," she said, reaching behind her to grip my arm. We followed the man, and Kit kept a tight hold on my fingers, so tight that I had to move her hand, holding it in mine as we moved past the reporters and were led farther down the hallway and into a small room near the back exit.

"Wait here," the man told us, then left, pulling the door shut behind him as he went.

"What the hell do you think..." Kit started, whirling on me as she paced. She was worked up, doing a lot of small, irritating things that were her usual way when she was nervous. But I didn't tell her to calm down or stop bouncing her foot when she leaned against one of the five round tables in the room. I thought maybe she'd work up some static electricity with the white and beige carpet from how quickly she paced, but I kept my suspicions to myself. Kit didn't need me telling her to calm down. That shit wasn't gonna happen no matter what I said.

"Did you..." she started to ask, going silent when I held up my hands, then gasping under her breath when the door behind us opened and the first lady and the president walked into the room. "Holy shi..." She went quiet when I nudged her, and then, just like that, on-air Kit showed up.

"Ms. Carlyle," the president greeted, offering his hand, which Kit took, looking composed, confident, though I did spot the quick shake in her fingers. He must have noticed it too, because the man held his free hand over Kit's as she shook, and he tilted his head, offering her a smile that was smooth, charming, but genuine. "And Mr. Kaino." He offered me a similar handshake, then introduced the first lady, who greeted us too. "My wife is a fan of your show."

"You're kidding," Kit said, a laugh in her tone that made me smile. She looked up at me, like she needed me to confirm what the president admitted.

"It's the ratings, Kit. Bill said they're big now."

"Of course they are," the first lady said, stepping forward. She had a wide smile, perfectly straight, white teeth, and from where I stood, the woman smelled incredible. I got a little star-struck watching her as she looked between me and Kit. That shit never happened. The first lady glanced at her husband and nodded at us. "Remember I told you about the show I watched where the people went into the homeless shelter and renovated it?" She looked back at Kit when the president nodded. "That was in Tacoma, right?"

"Yes," Kit said, head shaking like she couldn't believe what she was hearing. "It was my favorite project we've done. It meant the most."

"I could tell."

"Sir," the Secret Service man said behind us, drawing the attention of the president, who nodded at the man.

"Yes, well, we have to get going." Again, he offered his hand to Kit, then to me. "It was a pleasure to meet you both. I hope you'll keep doing the work that makes you happy."

"Yes," the first lady said, waving at a woman to her side. "Would you mind?" The assistant held up a cell phone, smiling at us.

"Not at all," I answered when Kit only stared back at the woman. "Come on, Kit. Stand by the president."

She moved like she was on autopilot, but she stood where directed, smiled when the assistant counted, and with just a few snaps of the camera and some parting words, the president and first lady and all the hangers-on behind them left the room.

Kit went on staring at the door for a long time after they left, and I smiled, head shaking as she stood there. "Eventually," I told her, leaning against the wall, "you're gonna have to blink, or your eyeballs will drop right out of your head."

"Kane." She exhaled, head in a constant shake as she turned to me. "That was the fucking president and first lady," she said, finally blinking.

"I caught that."

"They know we exist in the world." She moved close, eyelashes fluttering now.

"Figured that out when she asked for five hundred pictures and promised she'd tag you on Instagram."

"Kane…"

Finally, I pushed off the wall, nodding as she went on staring, not seeming capable of more than a few words.

"Come on, Kit. Let me take you to your car."

By the time we made it to the back entrance, the motorcade had vanished, the reporters had thinned out, but the crowd of hotel staff and curious onlookers had doubled in size. Kit followed behind me as I held tight to her wrist, relying on my size to part the crowd as we left the hotel and headed toward 6th Avenue and the parking garage.

We caught the attention of several groups as we moved, but no one bothered us, likely because Kit wore an expression that was a little giddy and ridiculous. She didn't seem able to make the wide smile leave her face, and I wondered how long it would take for her to let reality shift back into place.

"The President of the United States," I said when we were nearly to the parking garage. I dropped Kit's hand, and she walked at my side. "Was he everything you imagined?"

"Definitely."

"You on cloud nine?"

"Absolutely."

That made me laugh, and the sound of my voice brought Kit's attention to my face, made her laugh too. And as we came to the gray building up ahead and the garage entrance, that laughter seemed to relax her. Kit wrapped her arm around my waist and I let her, liking how good it felt to have her close, how normal it seemed to me.

"You know, I could go for..."

"Oh my God! It's you!" We heard behind us, and I walked faster, pulling Kit's arm from my waist to get us into the parking garage. "Hey, Kit! Kane, hold up a second."

"Fuck," I muttered, stopping when Kit turned. She held on to my wrist to get me to hold back and nudged my ribs.

"Ratings, remember?" she said behind her hand as two fans approached, both older ladies who looked to be in their sixties. They sported gray hair, the tips dyed pink, and stood in front of us, their phones already out from the fanny packs at their waist.

"Trust me," I whispered, "Bill won't know about this shit."

"I'm honestly on such a high right now I could smile for a thousand annoying fan pictures."

I liked seeing that smile. I liked how real Kit looked. I hadn't seen that from her since before Jess died. Right then, with her greeting the fans, answering the shit-ton of questions they threw at her, how Kit didn't bat an eye the more personal those questions got, I realized I'd do just about anything to keep that expression on her face. Even deal with overly curious fans.

"Kane, you're so handsome." The older woman winked at me, then seemed to think of something that made her laughter die. "Oh, Kit, I'm so sorry. That's so rude of me. I didn't mean to be disrespectful."

"It's not a problem," I said, leaning down for a third picture with her friend.

"No. No, it's not," she said, looking between me and Kit. "You know, we all saw that video." I glanced at Kit, surprised when she kept smiling, when that flicker in her eyes only got brighter. "Well, everyone saw it, didn't they?" The woman's laughter returned, and she tugged on her friend, pulling her away from me. "I think we should get a shot of just the two of you." She glanced between us, then at her friend. "That'll be lovely for the fan site, won't it, Ethel?"

"Oh, yes, Linda. You do a picture, and I'll take a video." Then Ethel widened her eyes, bouncing a little on her feet. "Oh lord, you know what would be great? If you two kissed. Oh, the fans would just die."

"Oh, honey, yes!" Linda took to bouncing like her friend, both old women moving closer, adjusting their phones as I stood still, my shoulders aching from the tension that had settled between them.

"I don't think..."

Kit cleared her throat, looking up at me, and I realized the request hadn't done anything to take the smile from her face. "Ratings," she mouthed, and then I faced her, forgetting for a second that we had an audience.

"You sure?" I asked her, thinking the spark in her eyes had gotten brighter. I wondered if it was the last-minute meeting with her hero that had given her the smile she wore, or if there was something more to it. I half wondered if I'd done something to contribute to it.

"The fans, you know," she said, her tone a little mocking. And when Kit's smile only widened, when she pushed against me like she'd been doing it for a lifetime, I decided I didn't care about the fans or the president or anything at all in the world but my friend and tasting her sweet mouth again.

It started slow, that kiss; a brush of our mouths, the smallest hint of wetness we shared. And then I inhaled, catching the hint of Kit's breath, that airy scent that made me a little drunk.

Next to us, I thought I heard the women laughing, making noises that I recognized as approval, but my mind was wrapped up in the taste of Kit and the feel of her against me, of her breath hot and damp against my lips, of her fingers sliding over the back of my neck. Then I held her face, covering most of it with my hands, enjoying her, all of her, for just a second.

Those vivid daydreams swam back into my head just then, and I didn't imagine faceless assholes who didn't know how to touch Kit. I saw myself touching her, taking everything she had, covering her body with mine, pushing apart her legs with my knees, diving in so deep that I got lost.

Distracted as I was by the taste and feel of her, I barely noticed when she started to pull away, and I opened my eyes, watching her, forgetting for a second that we weren't alone, that she wasn't mine to take like this. But logical thought went out the window. Reason left me completely. I wanted to keep on tasting her, and I was damn tired of pretending that Kit was only my friend.

"Kane..." she muttered, but anything else she might have said got lost when I pulled her closer, moving my hand to the back of her head, threading my fingers into her hair and diving back into that sweet, tempting mouth.

She let me.

Kit gave as good as she got, tongue and teeth and touches that were the sweetest tease. We got a little lost in the moment, my blood hot and burning me alive, and I liked the fire she set inside me and how it scorched. It was only the catcalling and old lady shrieks that broke us apart, though even that was a torturously slow movement.

I felt Kit freeze when the women started screaming, all giggling laughs and professions that we were scorching. "Holy shit!" one of them said, but I didn't look at her.

The small oath was enough to stop us, and I pulled back, still holding Kit's head, unable to do anything but look over her face, tempted to dive right back into where I'd just been.

"Well," Kit said, licking her lips, and that one word was enough to bring me back to myself.

"Hmm." It was no word at all; it was the same grunt of noise that tended to wiggle out of my throat anytime I was at a loss for dick-all to say. And I was, but I was also burning for my friend and eager to get away from our audience. "Ladies," I finally said, nodding to the old women as I led Kit to the garage entrance and straight for my truck.

She didn't speak at all as we got off the elevator and found my pickup. Kit didn't even remind me that she'd driven from Ashford and that her car was in the same garage. She didn't say anything at all as I opened the door for her, still trying like hell to get my blood to keep from burning me alive. Every inhale I released brought back the taste of Kit's lips and the memory of how warm her breath had been, how soft her tongue had been against mine.

We were out of the city and near a stretch of walking trails before I even realized where I was headed. My truck moved, I steered it, but in that cab, neither of us made a sound. Not until I spotted a long walking trail and a cluster of trees near the small parking area. I didn't think about doing it. Didn't use my blinker. One minute the thought of her over me, our bodies pressed together was in my head, then next I was hanging a right and finding two large Hemlock trees with limbs in need of a good cutting.

"Kane?" Kit said, finally speaking, finally doing more than looking out her window. "What are we doing here?"

I threw the truck into park and unbuckled my seat belt, debating what I wanted and what should be done. With any damn common sense, I would leave that truck, take a walk to cool down. Maybe run the trail just to get the taste of her out of my mouth, replace it with heavy breathing and sweat.

I had no damn common sense. Not when it came to Kit.

"Kane?" She repeated, then sat up straight when I leaned over to unbuckle her belt. "What are you doing?"

Kit was my friend. She meant a hell of a lot to me. She watched me at that moment as if I had answers she needed. As if anything I did would have to make sense. But I was out of answers. I was relegated to need.

"This," I told her, pushing the seat belt from her waist. It took exactly two seconds to lean toward her, pick her up, and settle her right over my lap. She felt warm, her light weight comforting. And then, I took her face between my hands and pulled her mouth to mine.

She released the smallest noise, half gasp, half moan until she responded, going at me like there was nothing left in her that wasn't primal and basic. It was fucking glorious.

"Kane," she panted, a low shift of noise that moved from her throat and turned into a moan when I pressed her against my throbbing cock. "God, Kane."

"Kit, kiss me," I told her, trying like hell to keep myself from losing it completely. I told myself I only wanted a taste, just that small reminder of what it felt like to kiss her, but fuck, it was hard to keep my control. "Kiss me," I told her again, "like you don't wanna stop."

"I...I don't..."

Yep.

Control.

Gone.

Kit rocked against me as I kissed her, pushing her down again and again on my cock, feeling that sweet warmth of her pussy as her skirt lifted higher and higher. I smoothed my hand over her ass, gripping the fabric, the tips of my fingers grazing the swell of her round ass.

"Ah..." she whined, grunting as I squeezed her ass, and I shuddered when she went at my neck, nibbling, biting, pulling my ear between her teeth, working her hips over me like she was fucking me silly.

"Want... Fuck, I want to taste you," I said, licking her neck, teeth against the tender skin of her collarbone, my free hand over her nipple. "Bet you taste sweet." I sucked on her bottom lip, grinding myself against her pussy. "Bet you taste sweet every fucking where, Kit."

I liked control when it came to sex. I liked to take and give and not be gentle. It turned me on to be in control, to have no inhibitions, to be free to fuck like I wanted. I'd thought about all of this, with Kit starring in my filthiest fantasies. But in that cab, with her rocking over me, with Kit's teeth and wet mouth drinking me up, I didn't give a shit about control. I didn't give a shit about doing anything but being with her however she wanted me.

"Kane...I want..."

My heart raced, and I felt my pulse throbbing in my neck. "Tell me what you want. Fucking please tell me what you want, Kit."

"Touch..." She shuddered against my thumb when I grazed her nipple. "Shit, Kane, I want you to touch me."

"Fuck..."

Sex was easy, and passion made you reckless. I could have moved her then, laid Kit on her back and fucked her raw in the cab of my truck. I could have gone balls deep, filling her up, touching and taking and having my fill because we both clearly wanted this shit to go down.

But as she moved against me, as I inched my fingers down her ass, to the curve of her legs, toward the sharp bone of her thigh, up to her damp thong, I realized what I wanted at that moment wasn't for anything to happen, but to see her fall apart. Not because I fucked her quick, but because I touched her right.

"You want my touch?" I asked against her ear, loving the sight of her features, how she sucked on her bottom lip, how my teasing touch over her thong, against her throbbing pussy, had her panting, moving against the tracing touch I gave her.

"Yeah...yes, I want you to touch me, Kane."

"Bad?" I said, frowning when I held my finger still and Kit moved down, catching my fingers between her pussy lips. "Christ..."

"Touch me, please," she said again, and I couldn't take how badly she shook, how small beads of sweat had started to collect along her forehead. "God, Kane, don't make me beg."

Even I wasn't that cruel. "Whatever you want..."

I watched my friend Kit shake, her nipples pebbling against her shirt, her body arching as I pushed her thong aside and felt her wet, warm pussy, as I slipped two fingers inside her and circled her clit with my thumb.

"You're so fucking tight, baby. So wet and warm."

"Yes," she said, her entire body shaking. I couldn't stop watching her, couldn't stop wanting to taste her, feel her. I could have come right then, just watching her as I touched her, as I filled her just a little.

"Squeeze against my fingers, Kit, squeeze tight and I'll make you come." I lifted up, leaning to kiss her neck as I worked her pussy, teasing, finger-fucking her until she was dripping, until those walls got tighter and tighter. "You like this? Feeling me inside you?"

"Kane," she panted, and I knew she was close. "Please."

"Please what, beautiful? I need you to tell me. What do you need?"

The loudest moan came when I sucked on Kit's nipple, teeth rubbing against that hard flesh. "Faster," she said, the words coming out in a pant. "And harder."

"Shit..."

No fucking way I'd deny her. No fucking way I'd be able to stay away from her or lie to myself about not wanting her, not needing her. I curled my hand, the knuckle hitting deep inside her, right against her G-spot, and I sped up the action, smiling as I heard Kit's breath go uneven, as she slammed her eyes shut and clamped that pussy around my fingers.

A few more swipes of my thumb against her clit and two fingers deep inside her and Kit shuddered, screaming a quick succession of "Yes, yes, yes!" before she came on my fingers, wetting my jeans and filling the cab of my truck with the smell of her body.

Nothing had ever been sweeter to me. Nothing would ever be again.

"Kane," she whimpered and fell against me, her body spent.

"I've got you, Kit," I told her, holding her close. "I've got you."

I fucking meant it.

Chapter Thirteen
Kit

"So, like, how good of a kisser is he?" Lexi, the hair stylist from the set, asked from the pedicure chair next to me.

I smiled but didn't answer as I wiggled my toes in the warm water.

Neva, our makeup artist, eyed me from the chair on my other side. She had that look again, the same one she gave me anytime she looked me over after she'd finished with my makeup. She was good at her job, and my skin had never been better. "Come on, Kit. Scale of one to ten."

"It wasn't a big deal," I lied. Twin eye rolls from the pair of them and I knew they'd called bullshit on my forced disinterest. My face heated, and the familiar blush crawled up my chest and neck.

"So, you only kissed him that one time in the bar?" I could feel Lexi's penetrating stare without having to glance in her direction.

"Maybe."

"Bitch, don't you lie to us," Neva said, slapping my arm as she laughed. "How many times have you kissed Kane?" The women never held back when we were alone, but neither of them had asked me anything until now.

I stared down at my feet, watching the water dance over the tops as the bubbles rose. "A few times."

"When was the last time?" Lexi asked.

"Yesterday," I answered truthfully because I knew these women. They'd badger me until I finally caved. Plus, they could spot a liar a mile away. Besides, the twenty different shades of red running over my face and neck would advertise any lie I attempted to tell.

"Girl," Neva drew out the word, being overdramatic like she often was. "We need all the details."

"Yeah. That man is a fine piece of ass, and he has some of the best damn lips. They gotta be soft."

My laugh was a little forced, a lot overdone because Lexi wasn't wrong at all. Kane's lips were out of this world, soft and thick too. They were made for kissing.

"They're pretty nice." I shrugged, hoping I could shove down the stupid smile that threatened to stretch across my mouth. Those lips were fucking spectacular, the best I'd ever laid mine on. When neither woman replied, I glanced from side to side and saw them staring at me, eyes narrowed. "What?"

"We want a play-by-play, and do *not* leave anything out."

"Fine," I groaned, but only because I was sick of holding everything in. Jess had been the only person I could talk about shit like this with. But she was gone now, and it wasn't like Kane would exactly be objective if I started going on about the kiss and hot make-out session. Hell, Jess would've known what I should do about whatever was happening between Kane and me. Without her here, I was lost.

"Start at the bar and don't stop," Lexi told me, settling back into her chair and making herself comfortable.

"I don't really remember the bar too well. I was drunk."

I had flashbacks, and the video Asher posted online helped fill in some of the blanks. There was no explanation for what had come over me. Kane had always been my friend, and I laid a lot of my shit on him when he didn't want it. He never complained, but we'd never once done anything similar to what happened at the bar.

A few drinks coupled with my messy emotions between losing Jess and flying high from our zip-lining, and I couldn't stop myself.

"We've all seen the video. You may skip it," Neva said, giving me a reprieve. "When was the next time?"

They'd keep asking. That was just how Neva and Lexi were, and for once, I was glad they were. Exhaling,

I sat up, rubbing my feet together in the water before I started.

"I needed him, because his brother totally flaked on me..."

I went into every detail. How we went from the president's speech, to the fans on the street, right down to where his hands had been, open mouth or closed, and how long the kiss lasted. I stopped at what had happened in his truck but had been generous with my descriptions of Kane's hands on my body, pulling me in for a deeper kiss, and how that small gesture had made me so fucking turned on I rubbed my hard nipples against his chest.

Lexi and Neva were practically on the edge of their seats by the time I finished. Their mouths were hanging open, and they were barely breathing.

"Satisfied?" I asked.

"God," Neva sighed. "That was *so* fucking hot."

"I knew I should've gone after that man as soon as I laid eyes on him," Lexi added. "Did you get to second base yet?"

I chewed my lip and went back to staring at my feet. "Kane would kill me just for telling you two about the kiss."

"Kane isn't here and doesn't have to know," Neva said, splashing the water in her footbath around.

"Maybe," I confessed. "But I don't know what to do about Kane."

Talking about what was happening between us wasn't easy. Especially after my little epiphany this morning while I showered. I stood under that spray for nearly forty-five minutes, reliving what happened in Kane's truck, remembering how much he had woken me up. That orgasm had been the best I'd ever had. His mouth, his fingers... Kane had done something to me I couldn't keep inside. There would be no pushing down my feelings. I couldn't ignore what I felt. It was like that orgasm had broken open a chasm of emotion, and it made me feel raw and free and unwilling to keep any of it silent and sleeping.

As I'd washed my hair and the hot water had made my skin pink and my body buzz, the realization hit me sweet and sharp and totally surprising: I loved Kane Kaino with everything I had.

But if Kane felt anything for me at all, he wasn't saying so. He only seemed willing to discuss the show. No emotions. No recollections about him making me come so loud I thought I'd rattled the windows in his truck. He'd gone quiet on me, and I felt like I was completely lost without any direction for what to do next.

"Ride him hard, girl. *Hard*," Neva said before laughing.

"He's my best friend, you know?"

Neva's smile fell, and she bunched her eyebrows as she watched me. "Doesn't matter. I have plenty of friends, and I've never kissed them. That's a pretty big step, even for best friends."

"Have you talked about it?" Lexi asked.

"No." I lowered in my chair, rubbing my temples. Kane had smiled when he'd dropped me off at my car in the parking garage. He even gave me a silent promise with one look when I'd asked him about helping me with all the items on the list. But this morning, he hadn't wanted to discuss what had happened. "He changes the subject."

"Here's the real question." Lexi straightened in her chair and stared me down. "Do you want to be more than friends?"

That was a very good question. I'd never really thought about becoming more with Kane because I worried it would ruin our friendship. I mean, not only were we best friends, we also worked with each other. I wanted more, but I didn't want to end up losing the last person on earth I felt I could count on either.

I placed my hands over my face and groaned into my palms. "Maybe. I don't know."

"That's a yes." Lexi tapped her finger against her chin as Neva and I stared at her, waiting for her sage words of advice. "Okay. So, you've kissed multiple times. You've been to second base, maybe more, but you aren't saying. I think that means a little more than friendship to both of you."

"You need to have a real talk with him, Kit. Or you're going to have to play dirty to get him to finally open up."

"Play dirty?" I glanced up, confused about how to play dirty when it came to Kane. The man knew me better than I knew myself sometimes.

Neva gave me a wicked smile. "You need to make him jealous."

"Kane's all about control. You need to make him claim you." Lexi giggled like a kid with a new toy. Or a Mean Girl with a new nerd to pick on. "He's like a caveman. Men haven't changed much in the last ten thousand years. Make him feel like he has to club you over the head and drag you back to his cave."

I laughed, imagining Kane with a club, trying any of that shit on me. He'd known better. I might be nice most of the time, but I had one hell of a punch.

"Yeah. You need to make him so jealous, he finally tells you how he feels or shows you," Neva agreed with Lexi.

"I don't even know where to start."

"We'll help," Lexi said and rubbed her hands together. "By the time we get back, you'll have an entire plan of action at your fingertips. We will not fail."

I wasn't sure what was the wiser emotion—fear or excitement. These two bitches were relentless and motivated. Maybe they were just bored, but as they grinned and rubbed their hands together, I realized what I felt most was anticipation.

Kane had given me more pleasure in a twenty-minute make-out session than anyone ever in my life. But it was more than that. He'd warned me about what he liked. He'd shown me something erotic, something sweet. And because it was Kane, because I wanted him and only him, I knew something had to give.

At that point, I would've tried anything to get Kane to commit to finishing my list. He didn't have to get down on one knee, but I'd at least like to have sex with someone I liked...or loved. And there was no one else in the world I loved more than Kane Kaino.

Chapter Fourteen
Kane

There was no excuse. That much I'd told my kid brother when he finally had balls enough to return my call.

"I had a source in Portland come through," he'd tried, and I wondered if he actually thought I gave a shit about his excuses.

When I didn't reply, offering only a low "Hmm" in answer, Kiel's voice got tight, forced.

"Look, Kane, I already told Kit what happened, and from what she said, it all worked out."

"Did she?"

"Well, yeah." He breathed, sounding irritated when I didn't speak. "Let me buy you a drink at Lucky's. I'll pick you up from the set."

I never said yes. Never said no either, and around four thirty, while the crew cleaned up for the day and Kit went off with the makeup girls for a late spa day in Tacoma, my brother's black Lincoln pulled into the drive.

I ignored the two taps of his horn and how he stood at his car, the door open, one foot still in the cab. "Kane?" he called, but I stayed inside the cabin, nodding to the hipster kid when he put the saws in the right spots for once and organized the extension cords. He was taking his damn time about it, but he was finally starting to come around.

Still hadn't attempted another mustache, though.

Another sound of the horn and the kid straightened, looking from me to the open door. "Somebody waiting on you?" I shifted my glance, taking my time with the last cup of coffee for the day. Asher, the hipster, only nodded, frowning again as the car door shut. "Some guy in a tie is walking up the drive."

"That right?"

"Yeah, and he looks..." He stopped speaking, watching me for a few seconds before he tossed the last extension cord into the duffle where Dale kept them. "Well, I suppose I'll take off."

"You do that."

There was a brief, full-second reprieve where I stood in the middle of the half-renovated cabin all on my own, before the crunch of gravel outside stopped and I caught the scent of my brother's expensive cologne burning in my sinuses.

"Fuck, Kane, what the hell?" he said behind me, walking inside with his hands on his hips, half looking at me, half glancing around the cabin. "I know you fucking heard me blowing my horn."

"Hmm."

"Fuck's sake," Kiel said, standing right in front of me. "I apologized to Kit. I apologized to you. I had work. Something that took priority…"

"Nothing," I said, finally looking at my brother, "and I mean, not a fucking thing, takes priority over Kit. Not when it's something that damn big."

Kiel watched me, eyes in a squint like he couldn't tell if I was fucking with him. "Holy shit, you are sprung as fuck."

"Go home, Kiel. I've got shit to do."

He followed me when I left the cabin, and I turned, waiting for my brother to leave the place before I closed the door, locking it up as he went on waiting for me to say something.

"You gonna give me the cold shoulder forever? That's mature, Kane. Seriously."

I shook my head, trying hard to remind myself that the beating he deserved couldn't be delivered on set. There were still stragglers moving around the trailers and lines of cameras placed around the property. I didn't need the hassle that would likely come to me if I was caught, yet again, on camera, doing shit I had no business doing.

I was nearly to my pickup before Kiel jogged next to me, pushing up the sleeves of his oxford so that the small tattoo on his forearm was visible. Sigma Nu. Stupid fraternity bullshit I told him not to get. Like most things, my kid brother didn't listen to me.

"Fuck, Kane, what's the big deal? You took care of it like you wanted."

"That's not—" I jerked around, readying to pummel him. I hated the little smirk that was always twitching over his lips, like he was constantly on the verge of cracking a smile. I stretched my neck, glancing at the horizon to keep myself calm before I looked at my brother. "Not the damn point. Of course, I took care of it. I always take care of shit when you flake out. Story of my life."

"Oh, give me a break," Kiel said, that smug grin gone now. "Don't act like you didn't enjoy playing the hero. *Especially* for Kit."

I took a step, fist curling at my side. "The hell is that supposed to mean?"

Kiel watched me, moving his head like he needed to give me the once-over before he elaborated. Instead of answering, my brother shook his head, and that smirk returned. "You want her. That's obvious." He paused, pressing his lips together before he continued. "I mean, I just wanna fuck her, but I guess you want that ass a lot more..."

I didn't think. I only saw blind rage, fury. It had left me after that time in my truck, with Kit's sweet pussy wrapped around my fingers, her over me, losing control. But Kiel didn't get to fucking twist that up for me. And he damn sure didn't get to say shit like that about Kit, especially not after what he'd done to her.

He barely moved when I went at him, tensing his body at the last minute before I punched him square in the nose. Once. I heard the crack of bone. But on the second punch, Kiel went down, falling onto his ass.

He held up his hand, covering his face to stop me before he scrambled to his feet. "Knew it! I fucking knew," he said, sounding like he had a cold. Blood poured from his nose, and he held a useless hand under his nostrils that didn't do anything but smear the blood over his face and across his fingers.

"Knew what, asshole?" I said, pushing him into my truck as I reached into the glove box. "Here." He took the Kleenex I handed him and tilted his head back.

"You love her." Love came out as "lub," but that wasn't what made me laugh.

"You're full of shit."

"Nope. You are." Kiel sat up, and more blood gushed from his nose. It didn't stop him. "I talk about fucking her, and you lose it. Broke my fucking nose. Stop being a pussy, and just admit you love her."

"She's my friend."

"Whom you want."

"That's not..."

"And love. Shit, you already admitted you're dumb about her. Just admit the truth." He jerked a second Kleenex out of my hand when I offered it to him and slid across my seat, leaning against the passenger door. "Such a punk."

"Says the asshole with the bloody nose." I glared at him, sighing when I spotted the blood on my leather seats. "Here," I told him, tossing an old flannel shirt at him. "You're cleaning that shit up."

"Fine. Just take me to the hospital, asshole."

I laughed to myself, but still got in, ignoring Kiel as he went on telling me what he thought I should do about Kit. His advice was stupid, some of it disgusting. And after a few minutes' drive, I tuned him out, feeling a little bit better after knocking him around. But as we moved through Ashford and my brother kept on spouting his bullshit advice, I couldn't help noticing the small knot that had started to form in my gut.

Kiel thought he knew the truth when I didn't know it myself. He thought he had a read on me when I wasn't even sure I knew who I was anymore at all.

That night after the president's speech, we'd both gone a little quiet, not saying much on the drive home. I'd brought her to the garage, and she followed me back to Ashford. The whole eighty miles, I watched her in my rearview, the cab of my truck filled with the smell of her, my fingers still warm from being inside her.

But I hadn't been able to say much about what had happened between us or what that meant.

"Will you still help me with the list?" she'd asked just before she left my truck in the parking garage.

"Of course I will," I'd told her, not real sure how I was supposed to act around her now.

"*Everything* on the list?"

No way would I answer that. No way could I deny my answer when I grinned at her, probably giving her a look that advertised what I wanted to do with her. Sex was on the table, for fucking sure, and as I drove home that night, thoughts of Kit and me together filled me up.

Kiel went on laughing at me, complaining about his nose and telling me what an asshole I was for beating on him over Kit. I didn't blame him for being mad, but I sure as shit wasn't happy that, of all the people in the world, my bastard kid brother was the one person who made me realize something that had been right in front of me all along: I fucking loved Kit Carlyle something fierce.

Chapter Fifteen
Kit

"Remember, don't deviate from the script," Neva said as she applied my red lip gloss. "You remember everything?"

I glanced up at her, smacking my lips together and trying to spread the stickiness out between both my lips. "I remember." Climbing out of the chair, I took one last look at myself in the mirror and knew that either the plan would set things into motion or would blow up in my face.

"You got this, Kit." Lexi bumped my shoulder, always filled with so much hopefulness. She was a die-hard romantic. Bet that crazy bitch was already planning our wedding.

That wasn't going to happen. When Lexi got that look in her eyes—all wedding magazines and trips to

David's Bridal—I shut her down real quick. It was a fool's hope, those wedding bells she heard. Because even if Kane slept with me and admitted to having feelings for me, I couldn't see either of us taking the plunge and walking down the aisle anytime soon.

"Make him jealous. If he ain't seeing red, up the stakes a little. Every man has a breaking point, even Kane."

"Oh lord," I mumbled before pushing open the door to the trailer and stepping outside. Lexi and Neva stood in the doorway, watching me as I walked across the yard toward the cabin.

"Sway your hips, girl!" Neva yelled behind me, and I cringed, hoping none of the crew heard her.

Activity swarmed in the cabin as the crew worked on finalizing the setup for today's segment. The remodel on the cabin was coming along nicely, and somehow, we were even on time. But that shouldn't be surprising. Kane always ran a tight ship, and it took damn near a catastrophe for us to fall behind. Even in my absence, the man kept everyone on task.

I bit down the quick lick of irritation that moved up my chest when Bill caught sight of me, walking across the room toward me and stepping over the small stacks of lumber that lay in his path. "Hey, sunshine."

"Hi, Bill." I tried to keep my tone light, welcoming, though it took effort. Bill wasn't my favorite person, hell, I didn't even like him, but I wasn't going to be a bitch to him. That wouldn't serve my purpose, despite the sleaze factor he had. He'd never cross a line with Kane always nearby. I figured if our show became big enough, we could request to have him replaced. It took clout in order to remove one of the most successful members from the team.

Kane was busy with Asher in the kitchen, but he glanced up, giving me a nod. I made eye contact but didn't so much as smile in his direction. *Play hard to get.* I let those little words play over and over again in my head as I stood there with Bill in front of me and Kane across the way.

"Have you been okay, Kit?"

"I'm fine. You?"

I was never one to make idle chitchat, especially with Bill. We had business meetings, always with other people, but we didn't talk much about our personal lives, and I liked it that way too.

"I feel like we haven't been able to really talk since the paparazzi started to camp out to catch another glimpse of the biggest *it* couple on television."

Kane moved a few feet closer, trying to be coy, but I could tell he was listening to my conversation with our producer. Kane was never too far away when Bill was near me, and it was obvious to everyone except Bill.

"We've all been swamped. Think nothing of it. I've been too busy lately anyway."

"What are you doing this weekend?"

Perfect opportunity to cast my bait. I took a glance at Kane, inwardly grinning at the frown on his face before I threw a smile at Bill, trying like hell not to vomit when I spotted the pit stains on his polo shirt. "Um, Seattle. I've got my eye on an antique armoire."

"Seattle, eh?"

"Yeah. I've been thinking about this piece of furniture for a while. It's more than I want to spend and farther than I wanted to travel, but…" I peered to my side, seeing Kane a little closer and quiet as he pretended to read something. "I don't want to go alone."

I set the first part of the "Make Kane Jealous" plan into action with the last statement. It wasn't a lie, and buying something I didn't need, something that expensive, would fulfill another item on the list. And, of course, it would serve a purpose. Lexi and Neva had convinced me that Bill would jump at the chance to go away with me. He'd probably offer to go away with any of the females on the set. The man really was a bad Hollywood cliché. We knew enough to stay away from him, but that didn't mean he wouldn't keep on trying.

"I'll take you," Bill said, standing right next to me. He smelled of coffee, sweat, and faded fabric softener. Not exactly a good combination. "I don't have anything planned this weekend."

I tried to pretend to be surprised by his offer and covered my mouth as if I were shocked, instead of trying to hide my smile. "You'd do that for me?"

"Kit, I'd do *anything* for you."

"You're the best." The words slid off my tongue surprisingly easy.

"I have a few contacts in Seattle who specialize in antiques. If you give me information on the item, I can place a few calls before we go. We'll use the trip to buy furniture for the cabin too so we can put it all on the expense account."

Kane came to stand at my side and cleared his throat. There wasn't a smile on his face or anything that looked remotely neutral. By the shift of his gaze between me and Bill and how tightly he clenched his jaw, I guessed he'd heard every word Bill and I exchanged before he decided to insert himself into our conversation. Bill was oblivious, but I didn't miss a beat when it came to Kane.

"Wow, you're amazing," I said with a big smile. "We can leave Friday after work."

"Where are we headed?" Kane asked, arms folded in front of his chest. He worked his jaw tighter, as though he needed to keep himself in check before he went all caveman and started beating on his extra-wide chest.

Bill narrowed his eyes, his frown telling me he didn't like Kane butting into our conversation or how he'd inserted himself into our plans. "*Kit* and *I* are going to Seattle."

"Where Kit goes, I go. I'll be ready to roll on Friday."

Kane didn't budge when I turned to face him. We hadn't argued. We hadn't had any problems as far as he knew, except that every time I mentioned what had happened in his truck, the man went silent as a grave. He might not know why I was irritated, but Kane would definitely pick up on my attitude. In fact, I counted on it.

"Maybe I don't want you to come." I crossed my arms, copying him, and stared Kane down.

The plan was going off perfectly. I couldn't have done a better job. Lexi and Neva said it would work, but I had my doubts. Sure, I felt like a juvenile brat playing this game with Kane, but my God, the man needed a nudge. He'd never make a move otherwise.

The years of observation between Neva and Lexi seemed to pay off. Kane's features hardened, and he grunted, cutting off the noise with a fake cough.

"Kit."

"Kane," I replied, not disguising my attitude.

"Kit," he said again, his jaw tightening further. "Can I talk to you for a minute?" Kane peered over at Bill, giving him the iciest look I'd ever seen cross his face. "Mind, Bill?"

"I'll let you two love birds talk. You're totally welcome to tag along, Kane."

"Thanks," he said in a clipped tone, but the word wasn't polite. In fact, it sounded a lot like a curse.

I stared up at Kane, watching him as he glared at Bill, waiting for him to be out of earshot. I wasn't stepping down right away. I planned to work his anger before finally "letting" him take me on the trip alone.

Kane peered down at me, his jaw still ticking in anger. We stayed like that, staring each other down for a solid ten seconds before he finally said something. "You aren't going away with him."

"Who says? You my daddy now too?" Behind Kane, I could see Neva and Lexi in the window, their faces practically pressed against the glass, watching the entire thing go down. By their expressions, they were pleased with my progress.

Kane moved his features into something resembling a clench—eyes hard and squinted, mouth tightened into a severe frown as he flared his nostrils. "Don't get smart with me."

I don't know why the exchange between us seemed hot, but it did. The bossy side of Kane, especially when he'd had his fingers buried deep inside me, did some wicked crazy shit to my libido, but I'd never admit that to him. The man was already unbearable at times, and that type of knowledge would give him an even bigger head than he already had.

I stepped closer, lowering my voice. "You didn't seriously just say that to me, did you?"

His stare then reminded me of the one Kiel had given me in the bar when I hugged him. But where Kane's kid brother had been seductive, smooth, Kane was pure alpha, gaze slipping over my face, eyebrow moving up like he thought things he wouldn't dare say aloud. That look felt like fire and lust and a hundred different filthy things I dreamed Kane wanted to do to me. That look made me realize Kiel was an amateur. Kane was the fucking master.

Just as quickly as he'd made it appear, Kane righted his expression, stepping back like he'd only just realized where we were and what he wanted. When he looked at me, the fire in eyes had been extinguished, and something worrying and tired replaced it. He reached back and rubbed his neck, finally breaking eye contact with me. "Kit, listen. You can't go away with Bill. I won't allow it."

"Give me one good reason."

The ball was officially in his court. He hadn't said anything to me about what happened between us. He'd spent the rest of the day pretending to be busy when he was ignoring my silent questions and stares. He'd acted like a worried big brother, but I wasn't his damn sister.

Right then, I felt like a motherfucker, and it was time for him to man up.

"You know he's a slimeball. He'll try to touch you and..."

I'd baited him. Now it was time for him to bite the hook. "And?" I raised an eyebrow, challenging the big, bad Kane to finally say the one thing I knew was on the tip of his tongue.

"I forbid it."

Laughter? Anger? I wasn't sure which emotion I felt first, but those three words left me a little speechless, and I was only able to gawk at him. The man just couldn't say the words, no matter what. He had to be the most aggravating and emotionally stunted human being on the planet.

Next to him, I looked like a character straight out of a Hallmark Channel movie, and I wasn't even very girlie or open with my heart.

I didn't respond right away. I stared him down, but when he didn't say another word, I stepped around him and headed straight for Bill, leaving Kane behind me.

"Book the rooms. We're on for this weekend, Bill."

Choke on that, Kane. If this blew up in my face, I'd have a bigger problem than being in love with Kane.

Chapter Sixteen
Kane

I wasn't a caveman. Well, at least, I didn't think I was. You can't be raised by a badass woman who handles two wild, ridiculous sons, a huge congregation of nieces and nephews, and still manages to cook, clean, make the money, and pay the bills all on her own, and somehow end up thinking you have any say in what a woman does. Especially when that woman isn't yours. Especially when you haven't told her you want her to be.

"Fuck."

The club was lousy with drunks, most of them, thank God, too damn twisted to recognize Kit or me. That still didn't make me relax, but then, relaxing had been the last damn thing I'd managed since we left Ashford.

The car ride with Kit and Bill had been the most awkward bullshit in my life. He flirted, moving his hand a little too close to her knee as he tapped the cupholder. She hadn't seemed to mind, something that irked me the whole way to the city. But then, I didn't care about that. Even managed a grin when Bill's fingers came too close to Kit's leg, and I stretched out my leg, weaving one foot between the two front seats. Cockblock executed.

I had no clue what I'd done to make Kit ask Bill for a ride to Seattle. One minute I had my fingers inside her, loving the feel of her sweet, soft skin all around me, the next she was ignoring me and flirting with the asshole we always made jokes about when we snuck off to the diner for lunch.

But Kit had spent most of the day after we'd gone to the president's speech with her girls in the makeup trailer, then the entire afternoon and night at a spa. So she said. Next day on set, I got the cold shoulder, and she was batting her damn eyes at that stupid fucker.

What the hell?

"I thought you hooked up with her," Dale had said, two minutes after Kit had stormed off and told Bill to book the rooms for the weekend trip.

"What?"

Dale couldn't have known. The guy didn't listen to gossip, especially not about me, and we both knew it. But the former SEAL had stood there on set, glancing between me, showcasing what was probably a stupid glare, complete with smoke funneling from my ears, and Kit, as she moved her hair behind her ear and gave Bill a smile I knew she reserved for people she was trying to charm.

"You and Kit? I hear tell there was a second kiss."

"The fuck, dude?" The admission had been the only thing that brought my attention away from Kit and Bill. Dale had grinned, shrugging like my question was pointless.

"Seriously, man...how can you work on TV and never pay attention to the shit the fans say about you? Don't you have an Instagram?"

That question had my mouth dropping open and my eyebrows going up. Dale seemed too gruff, too smart for stupidity like social media. "You do?"

He'd laughed, and I hated the tone behind it. Dale slapped my shoulder before he'd pulled out his phone, moving his thumb across the screen before he came to an app and a picture of him and four guys all decked out in desert fatigues.

"My brothers from our SEAL team are obsessed with Instagram. They think it's the only place to keep track of the women they have in different cities."

"But you're not active."

"No," he'd said, shoving his phone back into his pocket. "But those assholes still tag me in all the bullshit pictures they take." Dale had looked back at Kit, and the smile left his mouth. "Seriously, man, stop fucking around. That's two kisses that landed on the internet, and neither one was remotely innocent."

"How did you know about..."

Dale laughed again, punching my shoulder with a tap of his fist. "Fans, brother. They post everything. And you can't fake that shit you gave Kit after the president's speech. I might be a grumpy asshole, but I still got eyes in my head." He'd nodded to Kit before he picked up the tool belt next to his feet on the floor. "Woman like Kit ain't hard to read, and that..." He'd jerked his chin toward where Kit stood with Bill, too damn close for my liking. "That's a woman trying to get the man she wants to stake a claim." He'd moved away, fastening his belt before he called over his shoulder, "Don't fuck that shit up, Kane."

But I was. No matter how many times I reached between Kit and Bill when the guy made a move—my elbow knocking his drink over on the table, or my pointless questions to Kit about the kind of armoire she was looking for when we'd stopped in the antique shops Bill had picked out—I still wasn't getting any explanations from Kit. Or much respect from Bill.

"Kane, why don't you grab us a beer?" he'd said not five minutes ago when I'd asked Kit for the fourth time about the last armoire she'd checked out more than five hours before. Bill was a little buzzed. I could tell by the way he slouched against the table as he slipped me a twenty, and Kit was irritated either at me—nah, no way—or at Bill. Yep, that was likely.

"You volunteer me?" I asked the man, eyes squinting as I watched him. I wasn't an idiot. He had a plan. But then Kit sighed, slouching in her chair as another drunk tourist grabbed the karaoke mic and sang Gloria Gaynor's "I Will Survive."

Even if Dale was right and Kit was playing some stupid game, she was still annoyed. At me? At Bill? Who the fuck knew? I'd spent the day getting between them, not letting there be even a second of a chance for Bill to make a move. But then, I didn't take advantage of my upper hand either. It seemed that irritated Kit too.

Be cool, I told myself. *Calm the fuck down.*

I could do that. Pretend to cut my losses if only to get the frown off Kit's face.

"Fine," I told Bill when he didn't answer me, and I pushed back from the table, leaving the twenty where he put it. I leaned my elbows against the bar as I waited for the guy slinging shots to finish up with the three drunk tourists in front of him.

There was no mirror above the bar that would make spying on Kit and Bill easy, and there was no way to pretend not to be watching them without watching them at all. Instead, I lowered my head, pretending to study the tip of my boot with my face lowered, but my gaze shifted to the side. I stood up with a jerk when I spotted the table and Kit and Bill missing from it. I moved my head around the column that hid the bar from the section of tables, relaxing a little when I spotted Kit next to Bill on the stairs that led to the stage, talking to the tall guy with the braids who manned the karaoke shit.

It was on the list, I reminded myself. *Sing in front of a crowd of more than twenty people.* A quick glance around the club and I spotted more than fifty. Requirement met.

I could build her anything at all. I could demo a house in under four hours. I could jump from a plane or ride a bull if I were asked. Tires, carburetors, even the fucking tango, all that shit was easy for me. But singing? Hell no. I couldn't carry a tune in a steel bucket and damn sure not in front of a crowd. A man's gotta have some pride.

I was actually relieved she was tackling this item on her own. I'd heard Kit sing when she was piss-drunk and a good Patsy Cline song hit the radio. She was amazing. Of course she was. Maybe a little shy about how she sounded, but she was damn good.

The crowd would love her, and she'd love them right back without my making an ass of myself at all.

So why the hell was I frowning? Why did it feel like something thick and burning took root in my gut and was growing painful, sharp prickles?

Bill stood next to Kit, taking the mic, waving his hands around for the crowd to stand.

"Ladies and gentlemen, you're in for a treat! For one night only, here to sing with yours truly the classic Stevie Nicks and Tom Petty hit, 'Stop Draggin' My Heart Around,' is The Rehab Network's very own Kit Carlyle!"

The roar of applause was deafening, and soon a small group of people rushed to the front of the stage.

No one crowded her. No one tried to touch her, but as the music started and she began to sing, that prickling sensation in my gut got sharper. They all watched her like she was a rock star. They loved her, and she thrived on the attention. Kit flung her hair, motioning her arms, twisting the mic stand back and forth as she sang just like Stevie, and the crowd sang along, a loud chant of lyric and laughter the longer the song went on.

Bill wasn't half bad, I could at least give him that, but he was no Tom Petty, and he didn't have a tenth of Kit's charm. He could have been anyone. He was invisible, and if he touched her around the waist one more fucking time like he did just then, I'd make damn sure Bill disappeared.

But Kit handled him, pulling his arm from her body, playing to the crowd, leaning forward until she got to the line about needing someone to take care of you. Her gaze locked on to mine, her expression blank, but her eyes lit with something volcanic.

Then, the chorus. *Stop draggin' my heart around.* That shit was meant for me. She wanted me to get the message. I would have. The look on her face was warning enough, but then two drunk assholes jumped on the stage, moved Bill aside as Kit continued to sing, and I forgot about messages and meaning and everything else but protecting Kit from the groping hands of the bastards that danced on stage with her.

Being as big as I was made parting a crowd easy enough, but the job got harder when the crowd in question was filled with drunk assholes who wanted to laugh and dance and generally be a nuisance.

"Move," I tried several times, coming to a clogged table of shimmying females who couldn't be legal. Got through them with a little struggle, my focus on the stage and the biggest of the two numbnuts who had his hand on Kit's waist, pulling her back against his dick. "Fuck off," I told the kid when I got to the stage, sending the guy trying to pass himself off as security a glare that had the man stepping back. He had too much of a gut to be any real threat and didn't seem concerned enough to do anything when I jumped on the stage and pushed both idiots away from Kit.

"Kane!" I heard, then Kit screamed, both of us turning to watch one of the guys I'd just roughed up fall off the stage and into a throng of utterly wasted frat boys. "Oh God!" she said, scrambling toward the kid on the floor. She only stopped when I grabbed her arm, holding her back. "What the hell is wrong with you?"

"He had his hands all over you!" I told her, shooting a middle finger at one of the guys' friends when he picked up the kid from the floor. I spared half a glance at them both, then felt like shit when I spotted the kid's face. He couldn't have been more than eighteen and might have been a hundred and twenty-five pounds soaking wet.

"You didn't have to do that, asshole," his friend said, holding the guy around the shoulder.

"This will be bad if it gets out," Bill said, head shaking as he jumped from the stage and followed the kids across the bar as they left.

"Kane, what the hell is your problem?" Kit asked, tugging me off stage with a death grip on my wrist.

I couldn't keep my gaze from the kids across the bar and Bill's frantic gestures as he seemed to be trying to control the potential shitstorm.

"Kane?"

"I...I don't know," I told her, finally looking down at Kit's heart-shaped face. The tension in my shoulders went rigid, and I still felt that prickling sensation in my gut, only now it burned me with worry.

This was what I feared on the off times I thought about Kit and me together. Drama. Irrational reactions, all mine. Fucking complications.

"I don't know," I told her again, stepping out of her reach when she tried taking my arm. I waited for Bill to return, let him get halfway through the crowd before I finally shook my head, eyes squeezed tight. "I'm sorry. About...this," I said, waving toward the crowd before I looked at her again. "I'm sorry about fucking everything up." She knew what I meant. The disappointment came quick and sharpened her features. "I'll...see you in the morning," I told Kit, walking away from her just as Bill returned to her side.

There were groups of kids cloistered around the exits, all drunk and calling me an asshole as I moved through the crowd and out into the parking lot. Our hotel was only a block away, and I took that small walk to try to get the guilt I felt squashed down deep. It could go right next to the disappointment and worry I had any time I thought about Kit and me and how things had been before that damn list. Before that damn kiss.

No. That was a lie, I thought, just as I cleared the hotel's parking garage. I'd been twisted up about Kit for way longer than that. The kiss only made things worse, in the best possible way.

I leaned against the elevator door when it shut, head back, trying and failing to clear the look on Kit's face when I pushed that kid. Disappointment. Insult. I'd gone all caveman, despite anything I tried to tell myself about who I really was. Hell, I'd done that before we ever left for this fucking trip. My mom would whip my ass if she saw me.

"Shit," I said to the empty hallway when I left the elevator. My mom would whip my ass. I'd already ignored several messages from her about the video in the bar and me and Kit. I'd managed to put her off by claiming to be busy, and she'd been satisfied, only because I'd sent her a picture of Kit and me with the president and first lady. Mom was a little bit of a fangirl. But if anyone had caught me on film roughing up that poor kid and posted it... Five feet two or not, Mom would whip my ass.

Hell, everyone would. How bad would this be? I dropped my keys and wallet on the lounge table when I made it into my room, ready to drown myself in a shower by the time another round of guilt and pointless questions shot into my head.

Had Bill smoothed things over?

Worse still...had Kit gone to his room?

"Fuck!"

I stood under that steaming spray for a good twenty minutes, doing my best to let the stinging water punish me, wipe clear the bullshit mucking up my head, but it didn't work. Nothing would. Not unless I could apologize to Kit, something I considered as I slipped on my shorts and ran a towel over my wet hair.

Would she listen? Had I fucked things up for good? Would Kit...

The thunder of knocking on my hotel room door paused my train of thought, and I stepped to the door, forgetting I was half naked. Forgetting everything at all when I glimpsed the top of Kit's head through the peephole.

I threw open the door, resting my arms on the trim as I looked down at her, trying to ignore the sharp heat I swore I could feel as Kit moved her gaze all over my body. Just that look alone got to me. Each shift of her eyes over my thighs, up my stomach, to my chest and arms and back again, felt like a kiss, something hot and wet and sweet that I wanted from her. From only her.

But would that ever happen now?

"Kane?" Kit said, inhaling, small pink tongue sliding over her bottom lip like she wanted a taste of something that wasn't hers.

"Yeah?" I managed, unable to say more, that look she gave me taking up most of my attention.

"Let me...let me in," she said, stepping over the threshold. I couldn't move. It felt too good to have Kit so close, to feel the slip of her fingers against my chest as she touched me, likely trying to get me to step out of her way. "Let me in," she said again, and this time, her voice was low and sweet and fucking sinful. "There's something I want from you."

Chapter Seventeen
Kit

A girl could only take so much. This game was old, and I was tired of waiting for Kane to make a move. Little chickenshit Kit was gone, that much I was sure about the second I caught Kane's darkened eyes when he barely moved as I pushed my way into his room.

He stared down at me, and I wondered if he realized what message I'd tried to send him with this stupid plan. Hell, I'd been obvious. The song at the bar was very obvious too. "Stop Draggin' My Heart Around"? I mean, come on! I'd picked it to grab Kane's attention, and he knew I sang every word to him. The way he'd stalked toward the stage, eyes on me and the guys with the grabby hands, had my blood pumping and my heart pounding. I wasn't happy he'd practically pushed the kid off the stage, but I knew his heart was in the right place.

"What's wrong?" Kane stood before me wearing only a pair of thin shorts, tiny beads of water covering his chiseled chest. "Did I hurt the kid?"

"Fuck that kid, Kane. He was a punk. I'm not here to talk about him."

"Oh," he said and dragged his hands through his damp, messy hair.

That small movement caught my gaze, and I shifted it right to his chest. Maybe my stare lingered a little too long not to be noticeable as those muscles flexed with his movement. I'd seen Kane shirtless hundreds of times before, but tonight, in his room, knowing how he tasted, had me unable to stop what came out of my mouth next.

I swallowed once, inhaling to bring in the sweet, seductive scent of his body, and it bolstered me. I went for it.

"I'm done playing games, Kane. I thought you wanted me as much as I want you, but clearly, I've been wrong. I can't keep..."

He stalked forward, his eyes growing narrower with each step, but I held my ground, needing to say the speech I practiced on the way over here.

"I can't keep doing this."

Kane moved toward me like it was habit, some customary gesture that seemed comfortable and right. I wasn't nervous when he leaned forward, didn't shake or tremble when he placed his hand on my hip, his fingers digging into the skin just above my waistband.

"This?" he asked, that deep voice sounding like sex and sin in the quiet room.

"Pretending," I said, my voice a little breathless and definitely needier from the contact.

Kane didn't smile as he watched me, as he slid his hand around my waist before he flattened his palm on the middle of my lower back. "I've *never* pretended." He damn sure wasn't then, pulling me closer so our hips came together, close enough that I felt how hard, how heavy he was pressed against my stomach.

Back and forth. Yes and no. Fuck, but this man was confusing. He wanted me. I wasn't blind, but one minute he'd kiss me, act like a jealous fool when I mentioned someone else having me, the next he'd promise we'd never be good together. It all made me a little motion sick, and I jerked a glare up at him, angry and turned on, trying not to rub against him like a cat in heat.

"One minute you're kissing me, with your fingers deep and teasing, giving me the *best damn* orgasm of my life, and the next..."

He didn't let me finish, leaning forward, breath hot and sweet against my mouth. Kane tilted my head up, looking down at me like he wanted everything and all of me and didn't care that he'd left me confused. He watched me with half-lidded black eyes, sucking in his bottom lip like there was a small hesitation he needed to get rid of. I made a sound, something deep, hungry, and Kane flared his nostrils, licking his lips one last time before he stole my words and my breath with his kiss.

At first, it was gentle, a small graze of skin against skin. Sweet, actually. Then Kane curled his fingers in my hair, moaning low when I flicked my tongue against his lip, and he reached down, grabbing my ass with the hand that had been resting on my back seconds ago.

My reaction was instantaneous—hands on his forearms, fingertips inching up the rock-hard muscles before I gripped his biceps, curling around and tethering myself to him.

"Pretending?" he grunted, biting my bottom lip, groping my ass rougher and grinding his cock against me, which earned him another, louder moan I couldn't hold back.

He didn't need a response, and I kept a smartass reply to myself just then, so turned on when whatever clicked in Kane's brain or was some stupid response to the dumb "Make Kane Jealous" plan. I didn't give a shit what it was. I only knew I was finally getting Kane to touch me like I wanted. Like I damn well needed.

Kane swept his tongue across my bottom lip, and I opened for him, mouth dropped, body electrified by the sensation he kindled in me. Our breaths matched, pants filled with moans, with pleased sounds I hoped would only get louder, more eager. He moved his tongue deeper inside, fingers tightening as he tipped my head sideways, making way for him to deepen the kiss and have my knees wobbling in one quick move.

I slid my hand over his arm, kneading the muscles underneath before I curled my arms around his neck. I was drunk on him. A single kiss, the briefest desperate touch, his cock throbbing against my stomach, and I was already spent, turned on, worked up, and this wasn't even the most we'd done before. It just felt like the best.

As the kiss deepened, Kane trailed a path down my spine, the pressure of his fingertips growing more intense until his palm rested on my other ass cheek. I moaned my appreciation, almost begging him for more as I pushed myself against his hard-on, wanting so badly for him to be inside me.

I could have climbed him like a tree, I was that desperate, that greedy to be wrapped around him. I started to move, pushing my leg up, but Kane tucked his thumbs into the waistband of my pants and yanked them down to my ankles, palming my skin, skimming his fingers over my hips, around my ass before he squeezed me there, tight, needy. I broke our kiss for half a second, long enough to haul my shirt over my head and fling it to the floor. One glance at his face, at the tightening clench of his jaw, and I held my breath, ready for whatever he wanted to do to me. Kane grunted again, this time, sounding hungry, famished for me.

His hardened stare and ragged breathing faltered as he swept a gaze across my chest, to the black lace of my bra, over my stomach and the matching thong before he shot his focus back to my face. Kane breathed through his nose, reminding me of a bull ready to charge. Just the glint of hunger in his eyes and the way he moved close, pushing me against the wall, caging me with those massive arms, made my pussy throb with need.

"You wanna..." I exhaled, trying to get my breathing back to normal, loving the expression of dark need on his face. "You wanna fuck me, Kane?"

He didn't answer, but I caught the fists he made with his hands and shuddered when he moved his head in a long, slow nod. I stepped out of my pants and gasped when Kane pulled on the strap of my thong, slipping it down my legs, his mouth against my thighs, inhaling with each patch of skin he touched before he stood.

I licked my lips and reached for his shorts, expecting him to finally call things off. We'd never gotten his far.

Yeah, he'd had his fingers buried inside me, but we'd never been undressed in front of each other before and this close to having sex. My insides rejoiced, buzzing with excitement at the thought of Kane on top of me, driving me toward an orgasm unlike any other.

But Kane's eyes stayed locked on mine as I curled my fingers inside the elastic waistband of his black shorts. His expression was nothing short of unfettered need as the backs of my fingers slid against his warm skin. I went slow, liking the power I felt barely touching him, making his chest rise, making this big, strong alpha tighten his eyes as he moved his head, growling like a purring panther the more I teased his heavy cock.

"Kit..." His voice was lethal, sinister, a warning I took before I moved his shorts down, catching them with my toe to pull them off and drop them onto the floor behind us. I gasped as his cock sprang free, bobbing against my stomach, when Kane grabbed me, tugging off my bra, nibbling against my collarbone, then my shoulder.

My mouth watered at the contact, at the feel of our naked skin brushing together, the scent and sights overwhelming my senses and making the dull throb between my legs become almost painful.

I glanced up, taking in his entire body. The planes of his stomach were lined with more than a six-pack, which I'd never even realized was possible until now. His hard length waved again, teasing, promising how good he'd feel, giving me proof that all his alpha attitude wasn't because Kane was overcompensating for any shortcomings. No way this man and that long, thick cock were anything other than perfect.

He was *all* alpha.

Kane wrapped his arms around my waist, pulling me against his warm skin, only inches separating us as we stared at each other. He was giving me an out, I knew it. It was clear from how he watched me, moving his head to catch my gaze, sliding me against his dick to emphasize what was about to go down.

When I only smiled, shifting my hips so that my wet pussy lips slid against his cock, Kane crushed his lips to mine, rougher than before. He released a strangled grunt before he pushed me against the wall, lifting my body with his arm tucked under my ass. The painful pinch of the drywall at my back did nothing to slow the desire that had gone beyond the point of a slow simmer.

I flattened my spine against the wall and gripped his shoulders as I thrust my pussy forward, begging for more of his touch. The memories of the truck, his fingers pumping into me, had played on repeat in my mind, fueling every fantasy I'd had since. His grip tightened under my ass as he used his body as my support and pressed his palm against my stomach. I dug my fingernails into his skin and remembered the words he'd spoken to me. *I'm generous, but I'm not gentle.* Fuck, I hoped he was about to show me just how generous he could be. I could handle rough, as long as it was Kane dishing it out.

He kissed me, teasing me with the brush of his hard cock, breath heavy against my neck, tongue in my mouth, consuming me, and I couldn't take it for another second. Kane stilled when I wrapped my legs around his middle, pulling his cock closer to my center, silently begging him with a jerk of my hips. I wanted his roughness.

Who wanted gentle in a moment like this? Not me. I wasn't breakable, and I wanted to feel him deep inside, owned by the man who had been my best friend for years.

"I need you," I whispered against his lips, watching him closely, hoping he could see everything I felt in my features.

He grunted a response, slipping his hand down my middle and cupping my pussy in his palm. "This is mine." He curled his fingers, gripping me, possessing me. "No one else's. No more games."

I nodded, unable to speak, too overcome with emotion and need to trust my voice enough to form words.

My back bowed off the wall as Kane thrust two thick fingers deep inside me. I felt full, tight, and that warning he'd given me about not being gentle came to the front of my mind. He wasn't gentle. His movements were demanding, controlling, but felt fucking unreal. I wasn't leaving this room until Kane had more than fingers inside me.

He slid his tongue across mine, the rhythm matching the harsh strokes of his long, broad fingers as he pulled out before plunging them back, deeper and harder.

I inched my fingers up his shoulders before sliding them into the back of his hair, yanking at the silky strands between my fingertips. I lost my breath as he pressed a palm against my clit, the friction so delicious and rough with each thrust of his hand. My insides tightened around his fingers, the orgasm building quickly as his fingers swept against my G-spot.

I was about to come, everything inside my body tensed, when Kane pulled his hand away, leaving me completely empty and panting.

My eyes flew open, and anger flooded me. "What the fuck, Kane?" The rage was almost out of control from the orgasm that was about to break free. I gripped his hair with both hands, yanking back as hard as I could.

Had he changed his mind? Was he fucking with my head again? Christ, I'd kill him if he was backing out on the one thing we both knew we wanted.

I couldn't have been more wrong.

In one quick movement, Kane pulled me down on top of his length, spearing my body with his cock and rendering me stupid. I gasped, breath halted as he filled me so completely there wasn't even room for air in my lungs.

My grip on his hair loosened as he pressed his lips against my neck, licking the skin near my collarbone. His hands gripped my hips, pulling me down before lifting me back up, repeatedly pounding into me as our bodies collided. My tits bounced, scraping my nipples against the hardness of his chest.

I flattened my palms against the wall, steadying myself even though I knew Kane had complete control of my body. My breasts jutted out, pushing against his chest as my back bowed farther off the wall.

I blinked, head arching as I thought about what he was doing to me, smiling when I realized Kane was fucking me silly. All I could do was mumble as if I were doing an incantation and speaking in a foreign language only I knew how to translate.

Every time my body crashed into his, I was driven closer to the orgasm I needed and wanted so badly. My pussy clenched around his massive length, pulling him deeper and wanting everything he had to give.

As the orgasm grew closer, my entire body went rigid, and once again, I couldn't breathe. I squeezed my eyes shut, grunting more incoherent words as I tried to fill my lungs with air but failed.

Kane didn't ease up, thrusting his cock into me so hard that the back of my head started to bounce off the wall, but I didn't care if he knocked me out as long as I came before I blacked out.

"Yes. *Yes.*" The words I'd been unable to find before I came spilled out of me in a rush, my head buzzing as the orgasm I'd been feeling just out of reach started to build in my core, ready to ruin me forever.

"So. Fuckin'. Wet," he grunted, sounding awed, amazed, and the deep inflection in his tone had me wetter, crashing harder. "Fuck," he cried, fingers pinching into my ass, those low, wild noises he made sounding like music.

The last straw I needed was his teeth sinking into the skin near my shoulder, pushing me off the cliff that would send me into free fall. Kane tipped me over the edge and release crashed over me, over and over again as his strokes became more forceful and his fingers dug into my hips to the point of pleasurable pain.

I didn't know how long the orgasm sizzled through my system as Kane continued to pound into me, chasing his own pleasure. I only knew breathing was impossible and that I never, *ever* wanted him to stop fucking me. My entire body felt like jelly as my head continued to bang into the wall behind me. Then Kane moved his hand against the wall, catching my head, holding it still as he thrust harder, deeper, making me cry out again.

He wasn't gentle, but fuck, he *was* generous. That was the thing about Kane Kaino. That bastard was a man of his word.

"Take...take a breath," he said against my skin, moving us from the wall to lie on top of the bed.

"Why?" He started to move, and I pulled him back down, drying the small beads of sweat from his forehead. "Why do I need a breath?"

"Because, Kit," he said, licking my bottom lip before he pulled it between his teeth. "I'm not done fucking you."

Chapter Eighteen
Kane

Kit had a perfect ass. It was big and plump but still muscular, athletic. Fuck, I loved kissing it. Literally.

"Kane," she moaned, lifting her head over her shoulder, trying yet again to see what I was up to. Nosy woman.

"Hush," I told her, hand on her back, laying her down against the mattress. "This is my favorite view." I slipped a hand over her fine, wide ass, smiling at the jiggle when I nibbled the curve and ran my fingers around the bottom curve. "Fuck, you're sexy."

She started to laugh, a low, hot sound that got me hard, but being this close to her, having her facedown, pulling that gorgeous ass up close to my face was too damn much of a temptation.

I had to taste her. Every damn where.

The laugh died quickly when I lifted her ass, lowering my tongue over her pussy, licking her from behind because I could. Kit seemed to like that.

"Oh God!"

She tasted like fucking honey, sweet and warm, and every time I touched her with my cock or my tongue or my fingers, I got a response. Kit might be good at keeping whatever she felt off her face, but she was crap at staying quiet when she was turned on.

"Fuck, I could taste you forever." That shit wasn't a lie. She had a pretty pussy, all pink and tight, the lips small, her clit swollen and tempting. I bent back down to lick her again, lapping her over and over, spreading her lips apart to stick my tongue deep inside her. Then, I hummed against her, not able to keep myself quiet.

Delicious. Hot. Warm and fucking mine.

"Kane...what... Oh!"

She liked that, let out a little mew of surprise when I spread her cheeks apart to get in deeper. That small noise became a fucking whine of pleasure when I held her close against my mouth and slipped three fingers right inside her, teasing her G-spot until she bucked against my lips.

"Yes! Oh...yes, Kane!"

A few flicks of my knuckle in rapid succession against her sweet spot and Kit buried her face in the mattress, grabbing behind her for my arm, scratching and pinching my hand as she flooded my mouth with her orgasm.

She was wet everywhere now; on my mouth, on the sheets, and fuck me, was it hot. But I didn't give my Kit time to recover. I wanted her out of control. I wanted her crying my name, claiming me just as I'd claimed her.

"Get on your knees, baby." It took effort, but she complied, slouching against the pillow as I came up behind her. "Hmmm...*fuck*, Kit. You're so sexy." I grabbed that sweet ass, rubbing her lower back, kissing her beautiful skin as I slipped behind her.

"Kane..." She was already turned on, that wet pussy glistening as I grabbed my cock and ran the tip between those dripping lips. "Please," she said, throwing a glare my way. "I...I want you inside me."

"Fuck..." I couldn't take her saying things like that. Not since I'd waited so long to have her. One touch of hers and she owned me. Even if she didn't realize it, she fucking owned my soul.

Kit's entire body shook as I eased my cock inside her carefully, slow enough that she felt every inch I had for her. She hissed, gripping the pillow in front of her as she bounced back against me. "*God*...you fill me up...so much."

She went on saying shit like that and I'd be ruined. Already was. When Kit came into my room, when she announced she was tired of the fucking game we'd been playing, I decided I wouldn't even bother convincing her this shit might not work.

I kissed her because I wanted to. I fucked her because we both wanted it. And I kept fucking her because I didn't think it was possible to ever be full of Kit Carlyle.

I wouldn't stop wanting her. Ever.

"Kane, yes! Harder."

That shit fucked with my head. I'd always been rough with women, making sure they got enough from me, that they liked the things I did to them. Sometimes I could lose myself so much that they'd ask me to slow down or be softer. Never, not in twenty years, had I ever had a woman ask me to do her harder.

"Harder?" I said through a grunt, steadying Kit's body with my fingers digging into her hips.

"Yes. Hell yes," she said, rocking back so hard, taking me completely that I almost lost my balance.

"Kit...fucking hell..."

I grabbed her shoulder, moving her back, my balls tightening the faster she went, and I swore I saw stars when she clenched around my cock, milking me, gripping me until I could only rock faster, trying to give her everything I had without breaking her. I'd never hurt her. It just wasn't in me.

"There, Kane! Yes!"

Unbelievably, she came right there, with her treating my body like it was her plaything to be used for whatever she wanted.

Hell, who was I kidding? Of course it was.

She came for a long time, her shouts ringing out, becoming deafening, and I could only watch her, fascinated by how beautiful she was, by how much I still wanted her.

Nope, never getting my fill of Kit.

I was still rock hard, still pretending that I was all in control by the time Kit relaxed and pulled away from me, offering me her hand. She led me to the center of the bed, getting me flat on my back, her smile wide, a little devious, and I rested back against the pillows, still ready to go but curious. "What are you planning?" I asked, tucking my arm behind my head.

"Things..."

Kit straddled me, slipping her fingers around my cock, sliding them up and down while she hovered on top of me. Teasing, her wet lips against my tip, she watched me.

She held my attention with a small grin, with the glint of something fucking tempting in her eyes. I couldn't look away, couldn't decide what I liked more—her holding my cock against that pretty pussy or the look in her eyes that was all warning.

"Kit..."

"You're always rough. That's what you said." She closed her eyes, sliding herself against my dick, slipping it between her lips, making it disappear and reappear drenched with her wetness. "Have you ever tried being gentle?"

"No...not lately." My answer came out in a low moan, and I reached for her, frowning when she shook her head. "This isn't what gets me off."

Kit raised an eyebrow, looking at me, down at my raging hard cock, and then back up at my face. "Oh, really?"

I laughed, head shaking. "Fine, then. You want me to be gentle? I'll give it a shot."

"No, Kane," she said, coming up on her knees with my dick still between her fingers. "*I'm* going to be gentle with *you*."

Then Kit, my beautiful best friend, the only woman who could be soft and sweet and make me be the same and still turn me on doing it, slid right over my cock, burning me from the inside, taking me all without moving her gaze from my face.

"Slow," she said, moving, reaching up to rest her hands on my shoulder. "Slow and sweet and so gentle..."

I shut my eyes when she moved up, rocking back and forth, each movement tighter and tighter. "Oh God, Kane, gentle can be good." She leaned forward, taking my face between her hands, mouth eager, tongue hot as she kissed me, and I couldn't keep from being just as greedy. Fingers scratching along her shoulders, I held the back of her hair, not gripping but guiding her closer. I couldn't get enough of her mouth.

"Fuck, Kit, you feel good." She squeezed, going faster, nails digging into my shoulders again, and it felt like she was ripping me up, teasing and taking, and fuck if I didn't love every second of it. "Kit... God...I'm gonna come. Go...go faster." She did me one better. "Oh, fuck..." I mumbled when Kit got to her feet, squatting over me, using my shoulders to keep her steady. I held her ass, guiding, my chest tight, my balls tighter, and the only sound in that room was the low buzz from the next room over's TV and the slap of our skin as Kit fucked me.

Three long thrusts, each one a stab of pleasure that only got more intense, and I came hard, holding her against my cock, holding her like she was the only person who could keep me grounded to the earth.

When the aftershocks slowed, I wrapped Kit in my arms, loving how sticky and sweaty we were. I couldn't care less about the mess we'd made. I was in heaven, and nothing would take me from it.

"Kit..." I rubbed her back, kissing the top of her head. I wanted to stay like that with her, right in that spot, and tell the rest of the world to fuck off. I wanted it to be her and me and no one else for as long as we could manage it. "Christ, Kit..."

She rubbed her face against my chest, kissing along my pecs, grazing my nipple with her wet mouth before she exhaled, smiling at me, looking pleasantly fucked and a little smug about it.

"We made a mess," she said, waving a hand toward our bodies.

"Fuck yes, we did."

Kit started to move, and I tugged on her waist, pulling her back against me. "Don't leave yet."

"I'm sticky."

"I know." I rubbed a hand over her ass, giving her a squeeze. "I was there when it happened."

"Kane..." Just the tone of her voice had me worried enough that I didn't argue when she slipped off me and lay at my side.

I moved toward her, resting on an elbow to look down at her. "I do something wrong?"

"No," she said, fingering my chest again. I liked how she touched me like she did it without even thinking about it. "It's just...we've been fucking for hours now."

"Again, I was there." I kissed her nose, getting a laugh for my effort.

"I just mean...I'm good, you know. I'm on the shot, and I guess it's a lot late to even think about it, but..."

"Ah." I relaxed a little when I caught her meaning, but I still took a breath. Relinquishing this information did nothing for my rep or my pride. "I'm clean, Kit. I get checked every six months even though..." I shrugged, grabbing her hand.

"Even though what?"

She had pink polish on her nails; all trimmed, neat, and her fingers were small, dwarfed against my huge palm. I glanced up at her, shrugging. "Even though I haven't had sex in about three years."

"Wha..." She frowned, giving me a look that made me feel stupid.

"What can I say?" I kissed her fingers, rubbing my thumb over the knuckles. "I met this woman at my job and sort of carried a torch. Didn't have much interest in anyone but her."

Kit watched me for long enough that I wasn't sure my stupid confession hadn't cost me more than I thought. It unsettled me, getting that look from her. God only knew what she thought. When she didn't say anything, I fell back against the pillows, scrubbing my face.

"So, you haven't..." She moved closer, her naked breast against my arm. I shook my head, watching her closely as she looked at me. "No sex with anyone at all?" I waved my left hand, wiggling my fingers, and Kit laughed, pulling on my wrist to hold my hand. "But...I don't understand. Even if...that's a long time, Kane."

For a long time, I didn't say anything at all. Didn't much breathe either. Kit had a beautiful face and eyes that were round, hopeful. I'd always loved how open she was, how generous she was with everyone. I'd always wanted to make her smile, to be the one to make her laugh. But I'd never thought I'd have to admit the truth. Not really. I'd dreamed about this moment, about Kit and me together, naked, spent. But I'd always thought we'd skip the confessions. I'd thought it wouldn't be necessary.

I was wrong.

Kit deserved everything I had, even if that meant the things I kept wrapped up tight.

"Hell, Kit," I told her, keeping my voice quiet as I reached for her, thumb moving over her cheek. "I'm not a sad sack. It's just...when you love someone, everybody else is a cheap substitute." I sat up, kissing her forehead before I held her face still. "I only wanted the woman I loved. I only *ever* wanted you."

I'd made Kit laugh hundreds of times since we'd met. I'd seen her in a rage and ready to do battle when she didn't get what she thought she deserved from the network. I'd seen her sick and hungry and devastated by loss. I'd dried her tears before, but I had never put them there.

I did now. My small confession had Kit's eyes glassy and shining, and no matter how close I held her or how much I kissed her, those tears kept coming.

"Shit, baby, don't cry." She didn't stop, not even when I brought her against my chest. "Please, Kit...I'm sorry. Don't...don't cry..."

"I'm...I'm not," she lied, sniffling against my chest. "I'm just..." Kit looked up, wiping her eyes along the back of her hand. "God, Kane...I love you too."

I wasn't the kind of man who went in for hearts and flowers and big damn gestures that proved I loved someone. I'd probably fuck this thing up with her at some point, but right then, on that hotel mattress, with Kit looking at me like I was hers and she wasn't going to ever let me go, I swear to Christ, I could have written fucking sonnets and leapfrogged around Seattle just on the high those words Kit gave me.

Chapter Nineteen

Kit

Neva stood over me, pressing the matte powder against my skin with a hint of a smile. "You're looking completely refreshed after your trip to Seattle. Even your skin is glowing."

I'd tried to play it cool from the moment I walked into the hair and makeup trailer, but I was bursting at the seams to tell someone, especially the two girls who were more like my partners in crime than simply coworkers.

I pressed my fingers to my chest and glanced in the mirror, trying to catch a glimpse of the glow that I'd heard happened after someone had the best sex of their life.

"Am I?"

I turned my face, and I didn't see light radiating from my complexion. It was only me, a little happier than I was last week, and completely satisfied for the first time in longer than I could remember.

Neva pushed back a few strands of hair that had fallen over my shoulders and moved her face closer, getting a better look. The updo Lexi finished a few minutes ago was something straight out of a fashion magazine and a little too overdone for home improvement television, but I wasn't going to complain. "This love bite on your neck doesn't make it hard to understand why either."

My hand flew to my neck, covering the spot where Kane had bit down and sent me spiraling into a seemingly endless orgasm. That was damn sure unforgettable, but I didn't realize he left a mark. I hadn't even bothered to check before we left his hotel room to head back after Bill pounded on the door in a mad panic.

My eyes widened as I peered at Neva in the mirror, seeing the smirk on her face. "Shit. I didn't..."

Neva bumped my elbow with her hip and crossed her arms over her chest, raising an eyebrow. "You better start talking."

"I can't."

"Girl..."

Lexi walked up behind her, giving me the same look and standing just like Neva, arms crossed and waiting for me to spill the beans. "We don't have all day, and you didn't trip and bruise your neck, so don't give us a load of bullshit either."

"Fine," I groaned and dropped my hand from the spot I tried to hide, although I realized just then everyone had probably already seen it. "Can you at least cover it for the set, Neva?"

"You talk. I'll work." She reached over me to grab the concealer she'd already placed back in the makeup bin. "Don't leave a damn thing out."

I wasn't going to give them a play-by-play, but I could sprinkle in a few sexy details. Kane was a beast, everything I'd hoped and assumed he'd be. He didn't lie about not being gentle, but I loved the way he owned me. The generous part was no bullshit either, and besides using my favorite sex toy, I'd never come so many times one after another.

I hadn't answered right away, so Lexi being Lexi, decided to start with her line of questioning like I was in an interrogation. "Who made the first move?"

"Well, I sang karaoke."

"You did not." Neva gawked at me with her eyes as big as saucers. "And he still fucked you?"

"Yeah."

"That's like the kiss of death, girl. The man must really have it bad for you."

Lexi sat down in the chair next to me, watching me in the mirror. "Shut up, Neva. What did you sing?"

"Stop Draggin' My Heart Around."

"Shut up."

"She got some big lady balls, this one, Lexi, right?"

They laughed and I blushed. I'd known the move was risky, but it was easier to sing him the words than to keep beating around the bush. The trip to Seattle was about more than a piece of furniture. It was a "shit or get off the pot" type of thing, and I wasn't going to let Kane keep on insisting we were only friends anymore.

"Big." Lexi laughed, answering Neva before she nodded to me. "Keep going." She rolled her hand in a circle like I'd been the one to stop the conversation when it was entirely their fault.

"Anyway, after Kane knocked some poor kid off the stage—"

"What?"

"Shut up, Neva. You know Kane ain't going to let anyone touch what's his. Let her get to the good stuff already."

"So, after he stormed off and went back to his hotel room, I went after him."

"That's my girl."

Lexi gave Neva the same shut-the-fuck-up glare she'd just given her moments ago. "You interrupt one more time and I'm going to give you bangs, and we both know you don't look good with them."

Neva snarled but didn't say another word. I had to agree with Lexi. Neva looked like shit with bangs, and they weren't in style this season anyway. That much I knew just from hanging out with the girls because fashion in any form wasn't my thing.

"We have five minutes until Kane's here. You better talk fast." Lexi gave me a stern look, and I wondered if she was going to ask Kane the same questions she was asking me.

"I went to his room and pushed my way inside."

"You made the first move?" Neva slapped her hand over her mouth, knowing she was on the verge of losing some hair. She quickly snatched the scissors off the station and jammed them into her back pocket. "I'll shut up now."

I was laughing so hard at this point, I was practically in tears, but I kept talking before all hell broke loose between them. "I pushed my way inside and told him I was done playing games."

When I paused, remembering the way Kane stalked toward me and grabbed my hips before he kissed me, Lexi shook my chair, growing impatient. "Come on. Don't stop there, or I'll give you bangs too." She smiled playfully, knowing full well that my forehead was too short for bangs and I'd look like the world's biggest fashion don't if I had them.

"I told him I couldn't keep pretending."

"My girl. She's a genius." They both beamed like proud teachers, pleased that their student had successfully carried out the assignment without missing a single step.

"Bed?" Lexi raised an eyebrow.

"There was a bed in there somewhere," I said, smirking like an idiot remembering the way he did me.

"Where else?"

"Please don't say the floor. You know how unsanitary those hotel rooms can be," Neva said, scrunching her face.

"Neva, shut the fuck up. You've done it in the bathroom at a club. Can't be any place dirtier than there."

"Lexi, my love, I remember you banging that intern against the dumpster at the last remodel. Don't judge me."

I scrubbed my hands down my face, my cheeks aching from smiling so much at Lexi and Neva as they hurled insults back and forth like it was a sport.

"Did you get off?"

"I mean..." I paused and bit my lip because I wasn't sure how much detail I should tell them. They may never be able to look at Kane the same way again. "Well, yeah."

"More than once?"

"Oh, yeah."

"He a biter? Based on that mark on your neck, I'd say he's a rough one." Lexi bounced in her chair like she was riding a bull, bucking against the leather. "Damn that's hot."

"Yeah, I can't picture Kane gentle, and he doesn't seem like a missionary kinda guy either."

"He's definitely not."

All three of us giggled until Kane cleared his throat and closed the trailer door. We'd all been so engrossed in the conversation that I wasn't sure how long he'd been standing there.

"Oh, *hey*, Kane. We were just talking about Asher," Lexi said, trying to play it off, but based on the look on Kane's face, he'd heard more than we wanted him to.

"Umm-hmm," he muttered, walking toward the chair as Lexi scurried to her feet for Kane to sit down.

He glanced my way, shooting me a quick wink and a smile. I probably looked like a deer in headlights, freaked out that maybe I said too much and I wasn't sure how Kane would take us talking about our sex life.

"You ladies having a good morning?" Kane glanced at each of them in the mirror, throwing them his panty-melting smile, the one he pulled off without even trying.

"Yep." Lexi grabbed the clippers off her station but didn't look Kane in the eyes. "How about you? Have a nice trip?"

Neva sucked her lips into her mouth to stop herself from laughing. I gave her a *don't fucking do it* face in the mirror because I knew she was chomping at the bit to say something to him.

"Perfect."

Lexi smacked her lips together, fighting back a shit-eating grin. "We heard."

"And, ladies," Kane said, grinning from ear to ear. "Real men don't dig missionary."

My mouth dropped open, and I gripped the side of the chair, trying to stop myself from falling clean out of it. Kane had always been so private, but today, he was playful and willing to share more than I ever imagined.

Lexi and Neva glanced at each other, mouths hanging open and just as shocked as I was with Kane's statement. He, on the other hand, looked pleased that he was able to shut everyone up and gave them what they wanted with a single statement.

Kane Kaino never ceased to amaze me, changing into someone I hadn't seen before. He was playful and, dare I say, happier than I'd ever seen him before.

Epilogue

Kane

"So, let me see if I got this right..." Kiel stood with his hands in his pockets, squinting down across the boat as Kit got closer to the bow. There were two orcas twelve feet off the starboard side, and Kit looked ready to burst. But my baby brother didn't like what he saw. "You're gonna let your woman be handled by that asshole?" He nudged his chin up, gesturing toward the tour guide standing at Kit's side.

"What?" I asked, frowning when Kiel shook his head.

"The hell you mean, 'what'?" My brother frowned, arms folded tight as we watched the guide, a big guy, probably ten or so years younger than me and twice my size.

The smile hadn't left Kit's face since we first cleared the coast and the whales started surfacing. I'd have paid thousands more for a private tour, for a dozen more chances at Kit spotting those orcas just to keep that look on her face.

My kid brother though, for whatever reason, wasn't feeling our ocean adventure. "Look at that shit," he said, taking a step when the boat jostled and the guide held Kit around the waist.

"Hey," I told Kiel, stopping him with a hand to his shoulder. "Calm the fuck down. You'll ruin this trip for her if you start shit."

"You're serious?" he said, brushing off my fingers. "This asshole is working an angle with her, and you're just standing here like..."

"Like what?" I asked, folding my arms. There was a smile on my face too. It had been there for months, ever since that trip to the city with Bill. Didn't think there was anything that could wipe it from my mouth. "Like a guy who is happy his woman is thrilled she's ticking off the last item on her bucket list? Yeah. I'm just gonna stand here and let her have her fun." I sat down, winking at Kit when she waved at me, nodding for at least the twentieth time at the orcas. "Look at her. I haven't seen her smile like that since..." Kiel shot me a glance when I didn't elaborate, frowning like he was missing something, but I damn sure wasn't going to tell him about Kit and me and how we celebrated her finishing the half marathon.

Still daydream about that shit.

"You've changed," Kiel told me, and I rolled my eyes, waving him off.

It wasn't the first time he'd said that to me since Kit and I had decided to make things official. Not walk down the aisle official, but we had keys to each other's places in the city and toothbrushes we both kept in case of sleepovers. We weren't rushing. We were fucking basking.

"Maybe," I told him, stretching out my legs as I watched Kit take about the millionth picture of the whales. "But so the fuck what?"

Next to me, Kiel sighed, looking like a kid whose favorite superhero had gone all rogue and villainous. I grinned to myself, wondering what the asshole would do if I up and yelled "Hail, Hydra" at him.

"Listen, man, get used to it." I leaned back on my hands as Kiel looked out over the water. "Are you pissed because you didn't get a shot with her, or are you pissed because I'm not moping around miserable, pining after her?"

My brother shook his head and lowered his shoulders. "Neither." Kiel scrubbed his face, glancing once in my direction, but he didn't look at me straight on. "I...got offered a job."

"Yeah?"

He nodded, then sat up straight. "In...New York."

It took me a second to let the surprise wash over me, but when it did, I kept the complaints to myself. "That right?"

"I know what you're gonna say," he told me, looking at me.

"I got nothing to say."

My brother turned, body leaned toward me as he went on staring at Kit. "It was a long time ago, and she's nowhere near the city."

"That girl fucked with you."

He shook his head, rubbing his eyes as though just that small gesture would keep the memory of his ex out of his head. I'd seen my brother weak and stupid over women before, but shit, that particular chick had totally fucked him ragged.

"Like I said, it was a long time ago, and we've had zero contact." He finally glanced at me, relaxing the tension in his face. "I'm not a kid anymore, and this is a good opportunity for me. Great sources and a bump in pay. Besides, it's New York." He watched as Kit took a picture of the guide giving her a thumbs-up, one of the whales in the background dipping below the water's surface. "Going back to New York has always been the plan. Besides, you've got Kit."

I nodded, standing when the guide motioned for Kit to return to her seat. "I do," I said, pulling her to my side when she came next to me.

"You do what?"

"He's got you, Kit," Kiel said, rolling his eyes. "So he doesn't need me anymore."

I glared at my brother, laughing when he grinned at Kit like an asshole. "Like I needed him before."

"Before what?" Kit asked, ignoring Kiel when his cell rang and he turned toward the back of the boat.

"Nothing, baby." A sharp wind circled around us, and I pulled Kit closer, tugging my jacket open to cover her shoulders with it when she faced me, cheek against my chest. "You have fun?"

"It was the best." She gave me a squeeze, then turned her face to watch the water. "Best time I've ever had with my clothes on."

"Yeah?" I asked, laughing when I felt her smile against my collarbone.

"Oh, yeah, but it makes me a little sad."

"What does?"

Kit inhaled, stepping back a little to look up at me. "Jess's list. We're all finished. This was the last item."

I squinted down at her, running through all the things her cousin had wanted, each item completed, every one by Kit, with me tagging along, sometimes nagging her until it was done.

"Last one." I frowned, looking over her head as I held her close. "Well, actually, the last one was the most important."

"It was," she said, and the warmth from her mouth told me she couldn't keep from smiling. "And the best."

"You sure that's all? Every item done? Even that last one?"

Kit laughed, stepping back again to watch me. She pulled her hand free from the warmth of my jacket and ran her thumb along my bottom lip.

"She wanted me to fall in love. I think I did that a long time ago."

I had too, but there was no need to tell Kit that. She knew me well. She knew everything about waiting and needing and finally having what she wanted. We'd both done that.

"Well, now I think the real test should be the first item on a new list."

"What's that?" she asked, frowning when I only smiled at her.

"*Staying* in love."

Kit stretched up on her toes, kissing me slowly, the smallest tease that tasted like sugar on my tongue.

"That's not a challenge, Kane. Not for me."

"Me either, baby."

The End

Tied Down, Nailed Down #2, releases soon!
Visit chellebliss.com/nd for more information.
Turn the page for a sneak peek at Kiel!

Tied Down

SNEAK PEEK – COMING IN JUNE!
Preorder at chellebliss.com/nd

The woman two rows ahead of me knew she was beautiful. She knew how to work what the good Lord gave her. She also knew I was watching.

"Would you like another whiskey, Mr. Kaino?" It was only the soft twang in the flight attendant's voice that got my attention off the curvy brunette sitting front and center in first class.

"Please," I told her, not able to keep the wink from my eyelid. Couldn't keep from watching the woman's face as she leaned over my tray and topped up my drink. Smelled like peaches, all sweet and tantalizing, but I'd never been able to split my focus when it was caught. Just then, it stayed on that pair of legs at the front of the plane and the drop of one heel as the brunette slipped off her shoe. I liked the smooth curve of her legs. They were firm, the calves supple, strong. "Thank you."

The whiskey went down with a bite, something I found oddly comforting, something that did little to keep the swirl of arousal from my gut when the leggy brunette rubbed her ankle, thumb pressing down into the arch of her foot before she shifted a gaze over her shoulder, eyes lidded, fucking sexy and dark.

My brother Kane had schooled me about women. Especially women like this. But his opinions shifted to the old-school kind. He liked to play the protector. He liked to be straightforward, honest about what he wanted. But Kane was happily besotted back in Seattle with his love Kit Carlyle. And currently, the cable viewing audience and the rest of the country were taken by the PDA they displayed on their home improvement show.

Kane could have his woman and the happily ever after they were building together. Me? I liked to play. I liked the game, and I was a fucking ace at it.

I took in the look Legs gave, watched the slip of her small tongue against her bottom lip, spotted the tease of cleavage she gave me when she bent down, stretching to grab her shoe that had somehow ended up in the next row over. Accident, I'm sure. But deep down, I hoped she'd started the game—one I'd win. One that would end with me leaning back as that sexy woman rode me in the airport bathroom.

It would be a good way to welcome myself to New York. Celebrate in a JFK stall, maybe a service closet while no one was expecting me until the next morning. I shot a smile at the woman currently stretching, standing to the overhead compartment to retrieve something. Another play she made that told me she was a bit of an ace herself. She wore a fitted skirt and flowy blouse with a cinched waist. It made that glorious body look dangerous, and I was in the mood to be a little reckless. Legs looked around the cabin, shrugging to herself when no flight attendant approached, and pulled open the compartment, grabbing what looked like a small wallet.

She was out of the compartment in under a minute, but not before she turned to face me, adjusting something in her seat that brought her body facing me, her gaze jumping from the blanket she pretended to fix right to my face. I held that sharp gaze a full six seconds, examining the planes of her pretty face, the smooth, young skin, the pronounced angles of her chin and the thin top lip dwarfed by a bottom lip that had no business being that full and that damn sexy. Green eyes, from what I could make of them, and perfectly trimmed, arched brows. She was just this side of being too polished, too well put-together, but that only added to her appeal. I felt a deep-down craving to muss her perfect hair and smear her lipstick, all over my stomach and...

Legs stood straight, grabbing her small bag before she left her seat, hips in a tempting sway as she walked toward me. I got an up-close look, and my suspicions were confirmed: fucking glorious and gorgeous and *definitely* interested. No one looks at a perfect stranger the way she looked at me. Not unless they were attracted, and holy hell, did that look promise that she was a shit-ton more than attracted.

Her gaze went primal, hungry, and the way she let it glide over my face, right down to my lap, told me all I needed to know. She was biding her time. Maybe waiting for me to make a move, speak just a little to encourage her. But I was an ace, remember? You don't show your hand so soon after the game started.

When she swept by my seat, close enough to reach out and touch my shoulder, I moved, leaning back in my seat, smiling at the heat I felt from her stare as I closed my eyes. I caught her perfume as she moved by me —a fucking delicious scent that made me want to dive right between her thighs—and I licked my lips, wondering if she spotted the movement, hoping it frustrated her that I was playing distant.

The smell of her perfume disappeared, and I moved the smile off my face, making a mental note to thank my new boss Raquel for the shot at the crime beat in one of the most prestigious papers in the country *and* the first-class ticket. I felt like a king, comfortable, smug at having caught the attention of such a gorgeous woman, but then one of the flight attendants went around the plane, asking for final requests, and I knew we'd be landing soon.

Since I got the job offer, there'd been a bone-deep knowledge that something was off. Something that made me a little suspicious. I was a great writer. I was even better at researching and pressing leads for information. But I wasn't the best, not just yet. So why did I land this gig? And in New York of all places?

It was probably stupid to be paranoid. Likely even more asinine to listen to my big brother's warning before I left Seattle.

"Watch your back, Kiel. That family has a long reach."

He meant the Carellis. He meant the past.

Five years ago, Cara Carelli had jerked me into her criminal world with her mouth and hands, with her warm thighs and hotter pussy. She'd driven me away from who I was and any semblance of who I wanted to be. I loved her. I'd have done anything for her.

I'd been a punk kid just finishing up a journalism degree at NYU. She'd been the troubled source I ran into while trying to break a huge story. That story ended up with me getting the shit beat out of me and her brothers landing in jail. She'd told the cops I was a stalker. She told her family she didn't know me at all. None of those things was true.

I knew Cara. I knew exactly where she lived.

It took years for me to get my head on right. It took a lot of liquor and days of listening to my brother tell me what I'd done wrong and how not to do it again.

Cara had lied, and when I left New York after graduation, my killer story a bust, my heart ripped to shreds, I promised myself I'd never go back.

And here I was. About to land in the one place I told myself I never wanted to be again.

What the hell was I doing?

"You know," I heard, moving my head to the side when that familiar perfume filled my sinuses again. "I have a two-hour layover."

"Is that so?" I slid my arm behind my head, blinking my eyes open to see Legs staring down at me. She nodded, pressing her lips together, looking hungry. The brunette rested an arm on the headrest of my seat, and I pulled on her wrist, examining her left hand just to have something to do. She let me take her fingers, press them against my palm. Her skin was soft, supple like her body, and the nails were long, shaped but neat. "I might be able to help you fill your time." I sat up when she pulled her hand away, pretending to be a little wary of me. Then, when I turned toward her, resting on my elbow, she fought a smile. "I might be able to fill a few things."

A quick blush crept across her face, but she didn't frown or seem at all put off by my innuendo. I got a noncommittal shrug for my effort before Legs returned to her seat, shooting one final glance my way before the captain came on the overhead speaker informing everyone to return to their seats.

"Your glass, Mr. Kaino?" the flight attendant held out her hand, and I nodded, slamming back the contents of my whiskey, licking my lips clean before I handed over the glass, throwing the woman a wink for her trouble. But my head was still in the game and working out how to be smooth and subtle, just to see where Legs wanted to go.

Central Park was the first thing you spotted when you descended toward New York. It went on forever, miles and miles of lush green in the center of buildings that seemed to stretch and reach beyond anything you could see. There were skyscrapers and landmarks all clustered tightly together, and in the middle of all that, the massive park. Just the sight of it brought back picnics with Cara and the lies that spilled from her mouth easier than the wine that tipped from the half-empty bottle of Chianti.

Legs spared one final glance my way, eyebrows up in a silent question, and I grinned, moving my chin down to answer her. It was on, and I had every intention of starting my life in New York inside this beautiful, welcoming woman.

"Enjoy your stay," the flight attendant said, slipping something into my hand as I left the plane. I guessed what it was before I left the tarmac, fisting the wad of paper as I moved into the airport.

Legs was four feet in front of me, hips swaying, fluffing her hair as she moved toward baggage claim to grab her luggage. There was one small bag waiting for her. I didn't have anything but the duffle on my shoulder, and I waited, hanging back as she grabbed her suitcase, pretending to be more interested in my phone than the beautiful woman who slipped through the crowd, tossing a curious glance at me.

Kane had texted about my flight, and I winked at Legs, not watching the screen as I sent my brother a quick "just landed" text before I walked behind the woman, catching up to her as she headed toward a hallway sealed off with a "Employees Only" sign haphazardly taped to the wall. There were several cleaning carts and a few buckets around the hallway, but I focused on the slow tap of her heels and the roll of her suitcase wheels moving ahead of me and not the vacant hallway or abandoned cleaning equipment around us.

Legs disappeared into the last door on the left, and when I entered, the door still swishing closed as I came to it, that bone-deep worry returned.

The woman stood against an empty wall, hands tucked demurely behind her back as she waited for me. She'd already taken her shoes off and moved her bag to the side.

Two steps from her, I paused, securing her hand against my chest when she held up her palm. "How do you know about this place?"

Legs shrugged, and there was a playful smirk moving her top lip. "I know people."

"You don't know me," I told her, licking my lips when she curled her fingers around my collar.

"I'm about to."

A small release of sweet, bourbon-tinted breath and I grabbed Legs by the back of the neck, stumbling just a little when that full mouth dropped open and she offered me her tongue. She hummed against my mouth, seeming to get a thrill at how I held her, how tightly I fisted her skirt in between my fingers when she stepped closer.

"Shit...you taste so good," she told me, as though she was surprised, but she didn't pause for long and gripped my hair, moving my face closer, pressing her whole body against mine. "Better than I thought you would."

Her hair was thick, lush, and I twirled it between my fingers, using it to guide her head to the left as I licked a path along her neck. "You taste exactly like I thought you would. Sweet." I nibbled at the dip beneath her throat, then up to her ear. "Succulent." Teeth tugging on her lobe, I released the smallest growl. "Hot."

"Ah..."

Legs was a beautiful woman, and despite how my mother had raised me, despite what I knew was right and wrong, I was about to fuck her in an empty room at JFK airport. It made no sense to want this woman, but I did. She reminded me of...

"Antonia!" I heard, and the woman in my arms broke away from me, pushing me back against the wall like she wasn't supposed to be anywhere near me.

"I..."

Three oversized men stood in the center of the room, stoic and stern, but none of them had called her name. The sound of clicking heels met us between those men, and they broke apart, moving aside, and the clicking got louder.

Cara stood in front of us, looking fierce, looking more beautiful than I'd ever seen her, but she paid no attention to me. She glared at Legs, her face tight with anger. "I told you to get him here," she said, taking two more steps that put her right in front of us. "I never said you could try to fuck my husband."

Tension moved between my shoulders at the sound of her voice and that feeling I'd had all day burned inside my gut like a virus. Cara moved her head, gesturing for Legs to leave before she faced me. There was something cool and detached in her features, and just that look was warning enough. I should have bolted for the door. Fucking hell, I should have listened to my brother's warning.

But I hadn't, and just then, Cara faced me, keeping her features stern and her eyes dull.

"Hi, Kiel," she said, reaching out a hand to adjust my tie. "Welcome home."

About Eden Butler

Eden Butler is an editor and writer of Contemporary Romance novels and the nine-times great-granddaughter of an honest-to-God English pirate. This could explain her affinity for rule breaking and rum.

When she's not writing or wondering about her possibly Jack Sparrowesque ancestor, Eden patiently waits for her Hogwarts letter, edits, reads and spends way too much time watching rugby, Doctor Who and New Orleans Saints football.

She is currently living under teenage rule alongside her husband in southeast Louisiana.

JOIN EDEN'S NEWSLETTER
→ eepurl.com/VXQXD

FOLLOW EDEN ON BOOKBUB
→ bookbub.com/authors/eden-butler

Learn more at:
www.edenbutler.com

About Chelle Bliss

Chelle Bliss is the *USA Today* bestselling author of the Men of Inked and ALFA P.I. series. She hails from the Midwest but currently lives near the beach even though she hates sand. She's a full-time writer, time-waster extraordinaire, social media addict, coffee fiend, and ex-high school history teacher. She loves spending time with her two cats, alpha boyfriend, and chatting with readers. To learn more about Chelle, please visit her website.

JOIN CHELLE'S NEWSLETTER
→ chellebliss.com/news

FOLLOW CHELLE ON BOOKBUB
→ chellebliss.com/bb

Release Text Notifications (US only)
→ Text **ALPHAS** to **24587**

Want to drop me a line?
authorchellebliss@gmail.com

or visit:
www.chellebliss.com

Acknowledgements

From Chelle Bliss:

Thank you to Eden Butler for agreeing to write with me and helping my words come easy again. I've always adored your spirit and the beauty you portray on every page, sucking me into your worlds. It's an honor to call you a friend.

To my readers, thank you for diving into Kane and Kit. I can't even begin to explain how much fun they were to write, but don't worry... There's more to come.

And to the bloggers, you rocked it like always. Thanks for supporting our new series and we hope you loved every word Eden and I created.

From Eden Butler:

Thank you to Chelle for leading me into this journey. No one loves my words like you do. I will always be grateful for your love, support, and friendship.

To my reader group, the Saints & Sinners, my "sweet" team, and all the readers and blogs who continue to support my work, thank you so much.

And thanks, as always to my family: Chris, Trin, Faith, Grace, and Jax, for always loving me and believing in my work. I am truly blessed by such a phenomenal family.